Disco Mama

Tiffany Meuret

MOONSTRUCK BOOKS

ALSO BY TIFFANY MEURET

A Flood of Posies

Little Bird

Cataclysm

Moonstruck Books
Portland, Oregon
moonstruck-books.com

ISBN (paperback) 979-8-9888154-5-7

Cover design and interior formatting by FZ Boda
Proofreading by Amber Finnegan, Finnegan Editorial
Portrait by Eric Patton Photography

A NOTE TO THE READER

Be aware that some of the stories included in this book contain graphic descriptions of violence, emotional abuse, addiction, and other potentially triggering subjects. If you need help living, coping with trauma or harm, or staying sober, these resources offer support at no cost. Please reach out.

Suicide and Crisis Lifeline

988

The Rape, Abuse & Incest National Network (RAINN)

1-800-656-HOPE

The Trevor Project

1-866-488-7386

Alcoholics Anonymous

aa-intergroup.org/get-help-now

Adult Survivors of Child Abuse (ASCA)

info@ascasupport.org

415-937-1854

DEDICATION

To my children, whose impact on my mind, body, and soul is immeasurable. I lament the person I would have been without you.

Prologue

I have always had an insatiable appetite. As a kid, I ate an entire nylon jump rope, pulling it apart thread by thread and dangling its neon green fibers over my open mouth like a fish gulping air. My babysitter caught me, chastising me with my full name (Regina Gayle Clark!) but I lied straight to her face, claiming I'd been eating candy I stole from a jar on the counter.

I wasn't allowed sweets at her house for a week, but she never took the rope. By the time my punishment ended, nothing remained but two plastic handles.

They call my condition *pica*, but I don't eat inedible things anymore. I'm all grown up and all I want to do is lurk in dark corners, alone with my indigestion.

Tonight, the stage is yellow under the boring-bland incandescent lights. I mentally review the same setlist repeatedly, clenching and reviewing and clenching again. This show will be my crowning achievement. It must be–I've had little time for anything else lately. I lift my eyes just enough to wave at Cris, who is fiddling with the speakers. But soon my attention drifts inward again and

Cris disappears, everyone disappears, and the room may as well be empty.

My mind's eye begins the performance anew, and I hear it, I see it, and my heart skips because it's perfect. What a show. What an unforgettable show.

The people buzzing around me only look at me when they think I don't see them. The club staff thinks of me as a *condition*, something to be monitored, which I don't mind. Not really. They avoid all eye contact, staring instead at the bulbous lump of stomach resting in my lap. It's not a pregnancy, it's bigger than that, a distended mass I can only support by using my crossed legs as a scaffolding. Their nerves force an awkward silence that suits my agenda, my wishes for the human living inside of me. I have a show to prepare, and I need everyone to behave to execute it properly.

My stomach lurches with movement as the person inside of me claws at whatever muscle and tissue they can find in a furious bid for freedom. They're so eager for release they pulverize every organ within reach. Resting a palm to my skin, I shush them, promising that daylight awaits if they can only wait a little bit longer.

They respond in muted screams.

Chapter 1

Beginnings are difficult. How do you know when you're in one? Where is the beginning in the continuum of life? I guess it depends on the story you wish to tell. I think about beginnings on my way to work, or the grocery store, or the post office. All the boring places a person travels to in my neck of the woods, places that beget production. A person must be productive to be worth it; they must contribute. Otherwise, what the fuck are they even doing?

I'm in the car during this beginning, fumbling through my most repeated playlist at a stop light near Saguaro Park Boulevard. I am midway through my journey back to my house to retrieve my daughter Lola's school-issued tablet, which she's forgotten on the kitchen table. My boss might be irritated if I hadn't worked the same job for twenty years and earned enough seniority to slip away from my desk whenever I feel like it. I am productive, obviously, but never quite enough to be promoted. I once overheard Lola tell her friends I run the company, which is untrue. I never correct her, not even in private. Who cares what she says if it makes her feel better? Not like she has any presence of mind to know what being the boss means. If she did, she wouldn't glorify it to her friends, that's for sure.

Lola's tablet isn't on the table like her text said. I honestly feel a little stupid even looking there first–nothing is ever where Lola claims it to be. Her dad has a terminal case of scatterbrain himself, but Lola's case doesn't bother me as much. Maybe it should. She's seventeen and on the verge of womanhood. A better mother would have more concern about Lola's inability to care for herself–the child needs three alarms to remember to take her allergy meds in the morning–but I guess I don't worry for her as much as I used to. I should worry, most definitely, but I don't. I think I've just resigned myself to the idea that she'll live in a casita in my backyard until I either die or she burns the place down.

Finally, I find Lola's device under her pillow. Don't ask me why I even thought to check there, but that's where it was. Soon, I'm handing the tablet over to Shirley at the front desk at Ruth Bader Ginsburg High. They know me there. I'm kind of a big deal.

Shirley drops her head to the side as she takes the tablet from my impatient hands.

"She's still in gym," she says, and not a word more. Shirley has robust opinions about my parenting and my child, evident by the specific attention she pays to Lola's schedule. I figure that Shirley figures that *someone* ought to be looking out for this mess of a kid. And her messy mother–me.

I smile and thank her, just like I always do.

"Just doing my job," Shirley says, just like *she* always does. Sometimes I marvel at her dedication, but most of the time I feel sorry for her. She seems like a very boring person.

These near-constant interruptions to my day don't bother me like they ought to. Errand time is malleable–it can be pushed and pulled to fit any agenda. I don't have much of an agenda other than to maximize every second of freedom stupid enough to tangle itself in my clawed, old-crone hands. And I do the same thing with my stolen time, every time. I love the drive back–back home, back to work, wherever I am going. The drive back is the most unencumbered moment a modern woman could be gifted. No restrictions (the tablet is delivered), no time frame (the task could take fifteen minutes or thirty thanks to traffic, talkative staff, crying child, pick your poison), and no accountability (what sort of monster refuses a mother trying to help her child? She has an exam, *Cassandra*.)

Unlike earlier, I take my time selecting a playlist for the drive back. I love these interludes so much that I'll curate my queue to last the exact length of the trip. I make sure my Bluetooth properly connects before I put my eight-year-old Sorento into reverse, open my sunroof, and kick the bass to thirty (the highest setting in a Kia). Then I shred out of the parking lot like a teenage runaway and pretend, just for a few minutes, that I am anyone *but* who I am. The sight of me must be ridiculous, which I'll admit makes me self-conscious enough to turn down the volume long before I reach my parking space or driveway, but every moment before then feels like a dream. The beat of the music is like a heart palpitation, a too-powerful blast buried in my chest, a bomb screaming toward zero and ready to burst. Each track, a palate cleanser. Believe me, I am infinitely more productive because of these interruptions, and isn't productivity exactly what everyone wants from me anyway?

But just like every perfect moment, the drive back is fleeting, and soon I am installed at my desk, staring at a glowing wall of bolded, unread emails clogging my inbox. The ding of an internal chat tightens my jaw. I know without looking who it is from.

Cassandra Flanders <3
-Everything ok?

Cassandra works out of our company's southern office. Thankfully, it's a three-hour drive away, but that doesn't stop her from always knowing absolutely everything about everyone, down to their last shit; or from sending chats to remind her coworkers that she knows everything about everyone at all times. She has worked for the company for two years and it's been clear from day one that whoever isn't with her–like really *with* her, in the way that small dogs are *with* the one human they've decided to bond with–then they are against her.

Cassandra runs the social media and marketing department and has no problem with promoting herself, herself, herself. She even arranged a "surprise" birthday party for her own forty-third birthday three months ago. She pulled off this little coup by hijacking a Zoom meeting set up for the entire company to go over the next month's coupon promotions. Usually, coupon updates are an email. But for Cassandra, no opportunity to center herself goes unexploited.

The Zoom meeting was a horror show, a screen of false-stretched grins as my co-workers were each compelled to wish Cassandra happy birthday. I made sure to add my two cents, too. Although she did not appreciate being asked if she was dying–a valid question, in my opinion, because no one makes a big deal about forty-three unless they have something terminal. She pretended not to see my remark in the group chat, but I know she did because, again, Cassandra does not miss a thing.

Me :/
All good. Just kid things, you know?

I wonder if this will be the day when HR calls me in for getting in a digital bar fight with my work nemesis, but Cassandra leaves the chat unread, and I continue with my tasks until the day is over and the second best part of my daily twenty-hour cycle begins–the drive home.

The end of the day hits differently than its beginning. The drive home feels like defeat, like marching toward my own doom. Not like I don't enjoy being home–quite the contrary. I love being home more than almost anywhere else, just not on a workday. Workday evenings are work after work. It's a second shift that sucks the life out of me. Even if these evenings aren't busy, my thoughts are continually interrupted. I tend to be an irritable person anyway, but there is something so violating about being interrupted mid-thought.

As I drum my palms on the Sorento's steering wheel, I make the error of imagining my evenings as my own. When Lola was a toddler, she was an excitable banshee child hanging feral from my arms as I folded laundry, refusing to sleep without me laying with her and even then lying awake talking until midnight most of the time.

The advice then was always *you'll miss this when she's older*, which now that she's seventeen I can confirm is a lie. Sure, I miss parts of her toddlerhood, like her round, goldfish cheeks and her laugh and the cards she used to make for me nightly, stuck together by heart stickers I'd picked up from the dollar store on my way home from work. I do miss those parts, but the exhaustion? The screaming? No. Never. Any parent who has graduated from the toddler years and then had to babysit someone else's rugrat always thinks the same thing–how the fuck did I used to do this every day?

During Lola's toddler years, I used to daydream about my future self's evenings. I imagined what life would be like with an older child, one who could feed and dress and take care of herself, who cleaned her plate and did her homework in her room without any help. Now that I have this older kid, I can assert that she is just as frustrating as before if not worse, her helplessness now coupled with an utterly unearned air of maturity that demands continual argument. If anything, I am even more interrupted than before. I hold onto my unenthusiasm for the drive home. That is, until I arrive in my driveway, and the knot in my chest unravels at the sight of the pine tree in my front yard, and I think, "Thank God I am home," because I honestly never want to be anywhere else.

That's always been my problem, though–thinking too much.

Lola never acknowledges my entrance. I am so used to her ignoring me that I don't clock it. Maybe it's rude, or maybe she is just a teenager, but her ambivalence to me has never been a point of contention. She and I have an unspoken agreement, or at least I like to think we do:

we coexist, we acknowledge one another, and we interact, but only when necessary. In this way, she has never been more my kid.

My husband, on the other hand, has never understood how to act. His attention used to enrage me. I perceived it as a provocation, a greeting demanding a greeting, affection begging affection. It took years of counseling to understand that he was entirely sincere–an emotion eluding me my entire life because I would never dream of greeting another human at the door and meaning it. If I greet you at the door it's only because I need something or because I am mad at you. I believed my husband's genuine interest in my day was nothing but a lie until my therapist finally drilled into me that he was a different person who cared about different things, many of which would always seem foreign to me.

Learning about my husband's innate kindness made me feel like an asshole, because nothing interests me less than hearing about his silly, corporate day. It bugs me that we must discuss it even on a surface level. I hardly want to consider my own day, even less so his. But listening is what good wives do, and if I'm not a good wife then that means he is a good husband with a bad wife, and that would simply be intolerable because he deserves much better. So, I nod, and I listen to him chatter, and I nod some more as he slips his hand beneath my shoulder blade and guides me to an already brewed cup of coffee waiting for me on the kitchen table. Lola ignores me, not even a mention of my earlier act of heroism in rescuing her tablet. Not even a grunt of acknowledgement. Looks like this is going to be a very standard day.

The coffee is piping hot, doused only by a splash of whole milk, just how I like it.

"Oh, Jimothy, I don't know what I've done to deserve you," I say.

The name on my husband's birth certificate is not Jimothy, but I've called him that since we met. The name might very well be the reason we started dating, so, to me, he will always be Jimothy. Lola despises this pet name, so I make sure to enunciate it even harder when she's around. Sometimes it irks her, but not today. She's so intent on whatever she's doing on her phone that I don't think she hears me, but that's not new—with or without a screen.

"We're out of beans," he says. "I stopped on the way home to get some but all they had was Tim's Coffee Delight."

"You went into the office today?"

"Only for a meeting," he says, face plunged into the refrigerator. "Big waste of time. Clyde was there, too."

"At least Cassandra lives hours away. Lucky for me."

Jimothy releases the fridge door, and it shuts with a squelch. "You want burgers tonight?"

"Why not?"

"What about you, kid?" He waves a hand in Lola's direction.

"What?"

"I asked if you wanted a burger."

"What?"

"Lola, Jesus, look at me."

She looks up only to repeat herself again. Her third *what* was laced with a far more irritable tone than the first two.

"Burger. You. Lola. No? Yes?"

"You don't have to talk to me like I'm stupid."

"I'm not talking to you like you're stupid. I'm talking to you like you aren't listening to me. *Do you want a burger?*"

Lola rises from her bird-like squat on the stool. "No, okay?"

"You'll be hungry later."

Lola leaves the room without looking at either of us, nose all but smashed against the grubby screen of her phone. Her father's warning tails her exit like a bad stench, and then it's just the two of us.

"Should I start the fries?" I ask.

Jimothy nods, and we cook our meal in silence.

Chapter 2

As a kid, between years ten to fourteen, I would lay awake all night. I assume now it was because of some developmental glitch–a sudden explosion of brain growth while some hormonal soup soaked my gray matter in anxiety and sweat and self-awareness. I'd literally watch the minutes pass on my Nickelodeon alarm clock, *tick tick tick*, as one in the morning changed to two, two to three, three to a panic attack followed by dozing, and then suddenly it was daytime, and I'd be awake only three hours before I had to get up for school.

Those years were hellish for me. I considered everything. *Everything.* But sleeplessness is where creativity breeds. Navigating the night hours is a skill, something to practice. I had to cope with my insomnia loop somehow, so what I did was escape into myself. Instead of being stuck in a bed with a racing heart because it was too late–*too late*–to be awake, I was not. I was someone else, who lived anywhere but home. She was on an adventure, chasing a boy, slaying a dragon. Vaguely-Me could do whatever she wanted, and she did. Vaguely-Me shoved the kid that called me ugly right off his bike and into the gravel. Vaguely-Me was so enticing that her secret crush actually had a crush on her too. Vaguely-Me could summon bats. Vaguely-Me could live out every wildest dream, no matter how sinful or hedonistic, and she did. I learned to slip into whichever story arc tickled me when sleep was out of reach. Sometimes Vaguely-Me's exploits felt so real I preferred them to my waking life. I couldn't wait to go to bed so that I could think. So I could disappear.

This, however, did not solve my insomnia. Most of the time my fantasies made insomnia worse. I was so happy–satisfied, even–and sleeping killed it. So the hours passed, but I no longer watched the clock.

I sleep very well these days because I'm good at it and constantly exhausted. To close my eyes is to escape, and as an adult when I escape I also relax; and when I relax, I sleep. On the other hand, Jimothy can never sleep. Most nights he ends up on the couch because I snore too loud and it's so late that his brain will not shut off. He paces, stares at his phone, and takes sleeping pills, but his mind refuses to relent. On mornings following his worst nights, he wakes up in an accusatory mode, just pissed the fuck off that I can sleep and he can't.

"Like a light switch," he says. "Remarkable."

I nod and agree because it is remarkable.

This morning is another remarkable one, and Jimothy bemoans his aging back as he rises like a revived corpse from the couch.

"I slept like shit," he says, but I turn on the empty coffee grinder before he can continue, pretending to forget that we are out of beans. The noise breaks into Jimothy's complaining. Sometimes he just needs a little redirection.

"Damn," I say. "Guess I'm getting coffee on the way in." The hopper could be full and it wouldn't change the fact that I get coffee on the way to work every morning, regardless of whether I've made a pot at home beforehand. The only variable is the size of the cup.

Still, I start the grinder again, and then a third time, each rumble of the grinder's motor punctuated by a grunt from Jimothy. He knows what I'm up to and he doesn't like it one little bit.

Before I can continue, a door squeaks open upstairs and Lola screams in her pissed off, overtired teen way. "Mom! God, stop it!"

So I stop, but not without a deep twinge of resentment. This child should be kissing my feet that I lavish such respect upon her. I would never have spoken that way to my mother–I wouldn't dare. *My* mother never raised her voice. She didn't need to. She didn't beat me either; there was no need. *My* mother openly drank peppermint schnapps instead of coffee. *My* mother bought me nice clothes and was blacked out every night by six in the evening.

Sometimes I imagine my mother is still alive but is confined inside my head. It helps me maintain my perspective. Thinking of my mother helps me remember what not to be as I watch my own daughter drag herself out of the swampy waters I've held her head under since birth. My mother would have adored Lola–this I know–but not for any of the standard, wholesome reasons. The thought of my mother and my daughter having any kind of kinship withers all joy motherhood invites into my soul.

I may not know much about being a good mom, but I do know that the quickest way to get a teenager out of bed is white-hot frustration. I start the grinder again.

"You have school anyway," Jimothy calls to Lola, even though he might be angrier with me than she is. That's the other thing I know, though: the parents must remain united in front of the offspring. Outside of those two facts, I can confidently say I know nothing else about child-rearing. Lola has a way of sensing an abundance of confidence and shattering it at the tail like a Prince Rupert's drop.

Her door slams upstairs, followed by a series of thumps as our little princess tears through the clothes littering her bedroom floor like a rabid raccoon. It's been a minute since I've seen her do any laundry.

"Under ten," I say, and Jimothy shakes his head.

"She's mad, but just enough to get flustered. I say she'll be late for school."

We do this most mornings, bet how many minutes it will take Lola to get ready for school. Loser does the dishes. I can tell by Jimothy's clipped tone that he blames her predetermined, perpetual tardiness on me. He wishes I would stop antagonizing her like this, because it makes her moody and unpleasant. But Jimothy only has brothers. He's never had much interaction with teenage girls and fails to understand that absolutely nothing will stop them from being moody and unpleasant. It's nature. Beautiful in its way, if you know when to squint.

Exactly eight minutes later, Lola glides down the stairs. She wears no makeup and her hair is in a bun, looking like a million bucks. She bypassed her typical eyeliner just to flee the house all the sooner.

"Have a great day, honey!" I say, but she says goodbye to only her father and leaves.

Eyes on Jimothy, I tap my wrist where a watch might be if I wore one. "Under ten. I think I'll take a walk after dinner today."

I press the grinder's button one final time. "Don't forget we're low on dish soap."

Sometimes I wonder when everything went wrong. The one moment in which my future as I now know it was no longer malleable. Could have been when I was ten and decided to quit the softball team; or when I got pregnant at twenty-five; or maybe the defining moment could have been the weekend spent at the Children's Hospital when Lola was two because her asthma flared. Could have been when I decided to step down from management at work. Could have been when I forgot to pick Lola up from the bus stop in first grade because her early release slipped my mind. It could have been any of these moments or any one in between.

But those are the big milestones, miserable and sticky. A wiser part of me knows that the moment wasn't dramatic at all. It came on a morning four years earlier when I stood in my kitchen and realized I didn't recognize anyone anymore. Not my husband or my child, not even myself. I remember the relief as my chest unclenched for the first time in over a decade, the realization that Jimothy and I had done it, at least part way. We'd stopped our tiny human from trying to eat batteries or sprint into traffic–she'd lived, thrived! We'd all graduated to a new level of life. I left the house that morning positively euphoric. What a goddamn achievement, I thought. And then I plummeted.

It's amazing how we humans invest our entire beings into something–not because we love it, but because it's time consuming. We may resent the thing that defines our time, but all the same its absence rocks us like a death. 'Empty nest' is the term for mothers for when their children age. Mine showed up all at once, a sock to the gut. I have always been the mother of a small child. I was this mother up until the very moment I understood that I wasn't. Lola was still talking to me at least, but she no longer *needed* me the same way. And she never would again.

The drive today is quiet as I think. Sometimes I do that; I drive and I think, and my heart aches. I keep the tokens that both stoke and soothe my shame in the glove box. My sense of loneliness lures my fingers to them. Under the driver's manual is a worn manila folder whose edges are torn from my rabid abuse. Inside the folder are Lola's pictures and cards and letters. Rough drawings in scribbled crayon flutter out as I snatch the nearest page to me. I've restocked this folder many times, but my well has dried. Lola doesn't give me little gifts anymore.

The page in my hand is a marker drawing of an octopus. One from her later years, sixth grade or so, which was about when she stopped caring about drawing. This octopus is one of her monster creations. She used to regale me about them on her way home from school or after dinner. She had an entire codex of creatures she'd invented, each rooted in reality but with a twist. This octopus "excreetes poison from its tenticals." Lola has never been a great speller.

Someone honks behind me. The light is green. I hate myself for doing what I'm about to do, but also know I can't prevent it. Once my compulsion activates, not even

God could coax me away. So I hate myself for what I'm about to do, yes, but now I'll hate myself even more if I deny the urge. A person seeking a fix is guaranteed to ruin everyone's day, so for the sake of the humans around me, I pull into the gas station a few blocks over and park at a pump. The paper Lola drew on is coarse and stiff with age, the pencil descriptions faded from being roasted in my glove box for however long.

I trace the octopus's outline with an index finger and imagine what Lola might have looked like as she drew it–her tongue sticking out of her mouth as she concentrated (something she still does), apple cheeks blushed, adrenaline and excitement fueling her to completion. I see her holding it to the light for inspection and bounding down the stairs to deliver it. Maybe she gave it to me or maybe her dad, but it's with me now, and it is a marvel. Longing careens through my body because I know this is the last time I will look upon this forgotten piece of my daughter. Seconds later, I am tearing the paper into strips, eating each slice like they're squares of acid on my tongue. The paper dissolves quickly and coats the roof of my mouth with an invisible film that will linger the rest of the day. Scrap after scrap congeals in my throat, forming a thick paste of memories and regret.

Well, *regret* isn't quite right. Or maybe it is, but not for the reasons you'd think. In some ways, I do regret destroying a memory. I regret more the actual act of consumption, but the thing I regret most is the fact that I love every second of doing it.

I love how the drawing tastes–dirty, like cheap lipstick smeared on an old dollar bill. I love how it feels as it settles on my tongue. My body craves it, even knowing it doesn't belong; my salivary glands open in response to how the paper gradually dissolves and wilts, the slight resistance of crayon wax. I love knowing that something so precious exists only inside of me, both in my head and in my gut. No one will ever see it again.

Scanning the gas station for onlookers, I return the folder to the glove box, confident that I've not been seen. No matter the satisfaction derived from this subversive act, my insides vaporize at the thought of being caught. Not that anyone here knows me, or if they did would even suspect I was eating one of my daughter's childhood drawings. Still, my gut pulses shame like the neon sign of a strip club. *Looky here, perverts! Check this shit out.*

To date, the glove box holds the only remaining paper artifacts of Lola's youth. Perhaps Jimothy has a few tucked away, but if he does, he keeps them well hidden. Sometimes, I wonder if he knows about my habit, but the anxiety never lasts. He'd never be able to avoid bringing it up, tempting me into a confrontation. I suspect he assumes I throw everything away, which in many ways is so much more repulsive than the truth.

It won't be me who corrects him.

The rest of the day passes smoothly into evening, so much so that by sundown I'm sitting at our kitchen table with little recollection of how I got there. All I remember is the feel of paper on my tongue, laced with whiffs of gasoline. The sensation is so delightful that I refuse my usual dinner time cup of coffee, which obviously makes Jimothy feel some sort of way.

I ask, "Are you going to keep me in suspense, or shall I make something up until you're ready?"

He's hardly touched his food. Jimothy is a boisterous eater, even on a bad day. His shoulders droop over his half-eaten plate, an admission about to tumble out. I wasn't worried *per se*–Jimothy is generally a wholesome man, unable to keep a secret. An act truly terrible and rotten (divorce, affairs, money laundering type deals) doesn't even factor into my line of thinking. He certainly doesn't appear unhealthy in any sort of way, which leads me to one conclusion.

"Your mother?"

"Yes."

"What's wrong with Marilyn now?" I say just as Lola stomps down the stairs with her empty pasta bowl.

She eyes the two of us as she pauses at the kitchen sink. "What's going on?"

"Nothing," I say by instinct. It's an automatic response, always waiting in the chamber. "It's nothing."

"You always say it's nothing."

"And have I ever lied?"

Lola drops her bowl in the sink basin with an obnoxious clank. "I wouldn't know, now, would I?"

This is the shit that lights me up. This shit right here. It shouldn't set me off like it does because she's still a child, still too young to know anything, really, and this defiance is normal. But if Lola is the one to light the match, my dear husband is never far behind to touch the flame to the wick.

"Honey," he says, and it takes a moment to realize he's speaking to me. "It's fine. I was going to tell her, too."

Remember those two things I know about raising a teenager? Parents must always remain united in front of the offspring, and Jimothy has a nasty habit of confusing which woman in this house is his equal. He just detonates a bomb and leaves the cinders for me to clean up. Traitor.

"Jim-o-thy. Jimothy, really?"

"That's not even his name," Lola says.

Leveling a glare at Jimothy that I hope revisits his nightmares, I gesture for him to continue with my usual flair. *You see this? See what you've done now?* I've already forgotten he had something important to say.

"Why do you always act like this?" Lola continues. "He's just trying to talk to you."

I gather every reserve of patience at my disposal before answering her. "This does not concern you right now."

"Dad said it does."

"I am not going to keep arguing with you, Lola. Go to your room. Your dad can fetch you later."

"Mom–"

A surge of rage bubbles, too explosive to tamp down. My fist hits the table, hard. Plates rattle. Jimothy catches his cup before Diet Pepsi spills everywhere.

Lola freezes. I swear I see tears welling up before she turns away, but I might be projecting. She's stunned into silence for only a moment before she stomps up the stairs and slams the door.

"What the fuck?" Jimothy says. He's not looking for an answer. "Why are you two like this?"

I stare at this walking, talking idiot man, and stifle a scream. He truly doesn't see the role he plays. He thinks the tension between my daughter and I evolved completely separate from himself and his behavior. I can't hold it in anymore. I'm going to scream; I swear to God if he says one more thing I'm going to–

"My mom is dying."

Well.

"Rapid onset dementia. There's no one else. I have to go." When he says there's no one else, he means that he is the only brother left who will speak to her. When he says he has to go, he means to Utah.

"How long?" I'm hoping he stays for a week. Maybe two. Just to get Marilyn settled in a facility, but the way his shoulders droop further snips any thread of hope on which I might hang my delusion.

"There's the house, her effects, end-of-life planning, getting her into treatment. I mean, it could be...I don't know."

Goddamn it. "How long?"

"At least a month."

When he says at least a month, he means many months. This should be fine. I am a grown woman and Lola isn't a baby, but dread curdles in my gut as the implications take hold.

It's going to be just me and Lola. For *months*.

My anxiety must be evident, because he scoops my hand into his, rubbing my palm with his thumb. "Maybe this will be good for you two."

All my strained frustration wilts into terror. I like to think Jimothy creates more tension than he solves, that he causes this rift between myself and my daughter, but we both know this isn't true. He may be clueless sometimes, but without him Lola and I would have destroyed each other long before she reached her teens.

"When do you leave?"

"There are some flights leaving as soon as tomorrow."

"God, is Marilyn really that bad?" I feel like a bitch for asking, but I need him to tell me clearly and in no uncertain terms that there is no way around this. If he doesn't, I'll resent him for everything that could possibly go wrong in his absence. Not my finest quality, but what can you do?

Jimothy rubs his temples, a sure sign he's had quite enough of me. "She left her house yesterday, God knows why–to get the mail, maybe–and the police found her ten miles from home, barefoot."

"Jesus Christ." That *is* bad. Very bad. Tomorrow might not be soon enough. "You have to go right away. Fuck."

He squeezes my hand, a slight smile breaking his otherwise somber exterior. "You're going to be fine," he says.

Somewhere upstairs, the door to the bathroom slams.

Neither of us say another word.

Chapter 3

This night feels like those desperate nights when my brain continually spins on its axis until morning, incapable of rest. I sneak around the house a lot, especially around my teenage daughter, avoiding our volatile skirmishes. I pace the house once an hour, unable to settle, until I finally cave to my compulsion and tiptoe up to Lola's room.

Lola never did like a night light like other kids. Her room is pitch black but my eyes quickly adjust. My darling sleeps with the same temperament as she lives–irritated and uncomfortable. Her arms flail about, never settled, never comfortable, and she talks a lot. Sometimes she whimpers like an infant, which makes me yearn to touch her, calm her, soothe her like any mother soothes her wailing newborn, but that would be a grave error. Lola wakes at the smallest of noises, just like her dad. Should I disrupt even a strand of hair, she'd jerk upright in a fury. Ask me how I know.

So instead, I watch her and remember how she once was, even though she's alive and thriving and breathing right in front of me. Night is the only time she allows me to see peace on her face. Looking at her sleep, I remember her younger self. And in my hands, I twist a piece of her baby blanket, the one she told me to throw away when she was eight years old because she was suddenly and immediately too big for a blankie, and I shred the threads between my restless nails. Periwinkle fibers glide to my feet, light as feathers. The blankie is nearly gone, eroded by my anxiety. I want to touch Lola's cheek, maybe run my fingers through her hair, but I don't because she'll hate me for it, and then this tender moment will fade into fury as Lola catches me adoring her in the dark. She's peaceful when she doesn't think I'm around. I'm peaceful when she's unconscious.

Only once the shadows shift do I leave her room. It's somehow five in the morning and my back screams from standing still for so long. I greet Jimothy with a fresh cup of coffee before he leaves for his flight to Utah. Lola doesn't come out of her room. She might be sleeping, but I think she's angry at him for leaving so suddenly–angry because he is leaving her with *me*.

❖ ❖ ❖

Our first few days without Jimothy run smoothly, mainly because we each keep to our respective quarters. Jimothy calls to update me nightly, while texting his daughter that he misses her already; his persistence makes me think that he's trying to get a feel for how we're managing on our own. Lola goes to school, I go to work. She takes dinner to her room, and I don't pressure her to eat with me. I clean the kitchen with my music on too loud, she texts me to please turn it down, and I do, barely. We are doing just fine–until we are not.

The night that changes our dynamic begins when Lola approaches me with an odd aura of civility. Her features are soft, not creased and pinched and scowling, and she sits next to me at the table while I'm chewing my microwave enchilada. She folds her hands on the table in front of her. She couldn't behave more obviously if she tried.

"There's more if you're hungry," I say, understanding full well she is not looking for anything to eat.

"Emily texted me," she starts. I notice a spot of blood on her middle finger. She's been picking at her cuticles again.

"Her dad is taking her and Lisha to the Rat House for a show. It's small. Emily's cousin is in a band, and they're terrible, Mom. Real shit. They've asked me to come tonight so there'll at least be some friendly faces. They're gonna crash and burn, I swear it's going to be so bad, and it would be super nice for them to have, like, fans or something? I don't know. But I'll be home early, like midnight at the latest, and Emily's dad will be there the entire time. So, what do you think?"

Calmly, and I must emphasize my calm here, I drop my fork to my plate. "Excuse me, but did you just ask me to go to a place called the *Rat* House?"

Lola threatens to hurl her angst into a prolonged *Moooom* but catches herself just in time. "It's just a dumb name. It doesn't mean anything."

"Ahh, yes, the Rat House, notorious for their late-night SAT prep courses."

"Mom—"

I'm not sure what comes over me. I should nip this in the bud, I think, as I hold up my hand. Maybe I'm just bored, or perhaps Lola finally won and I'm just too tired to argue, but I say the words the me of two minutes ago would find ridiculous. "You can go."

Lola is so used to arguing with me that it takes a second for her ready-made grimace to unwind into a smile. "Are you serious? I can go? Oh my *God*, Mom, you are the best. I swear. Thank you!"

She beams–she's luminous–and for a second everything feels right again. My daughter thinks I'm cool. She *hugs* me, for fuck's sake. She's so excited that she doesn't notice the way I run my fingers through her curls as I hug her back. How long since she's hugged me and meant it? More than a year. And then she's up the stairs to change, text notifications pinging incessantly. I hear a muffled squeal, and I'm alone again with my cooling enchilada I probably was never going to finish anyway.

Only then do I realize what I've agreed to. My seventeen-year-old daughter is going to the Rat House. Where the fuck is the Rat House? She didn't even say which part of town she'd be traveling to. Lola certainly doesn't have any money, so what will she do if there's a cover charge? Flash her underage tits for the bouncer? What have I done?

I consider, however briefly, rescinding my approval. The potential weight of Jimothy's disapproval alone drains the blood from my cheeks. But then Lola is bounding down the stairs with the glee she had as a toddler, momentum more powerful than her feet, and I know I can't. I just can't. She's put on blue eye shadow and a band t-shirt that reads Beefy Reefer and I curdle inside as I realize again that I've just signed off on this awful, awful adventure. God, is the cousin's band called Beefy Reefer? Fucking kill me.

"Where is this place," I ask before she can fully escape the house. She's got one foot on the stoop. Freezes. She was probably praying I wouldn't ask.

"Midtown," she says. "You can google it. I'll have my phone the entire time! Bye, Mom, thank you!"

Then she's gone. My dinner is cold. My child is going to see Beefy Reefer with her dumbass friends and I just let it happen. In the silence after Lola's departure, I realize I could bet my right hand that Emily's dad was never escorting them.

Goddamn it.

❖ ❖ ❖

The Rat House is even worse than I imagined. The building sits at the end of a dark alley like a canker sore, offensively out of place. The fluorescent bulbs of the sign's H and O are burnt out and the exterior is straight out of an apocalypse, a shoebox hole for degenerates and runaways and terrible bands–the kind of place where the booze is well liquor and the best weed you'll ever smoke is sold out of the women's bathroom. It's exactly the sort of place I would have loved in my twenties, which only exacerbates my anxiety.

Sitting in my car, I consider how to even get close to the building without being spotted. Lola will be furious to know I've followed her–absolutely livid and offended. I don't particularly want to deal with that tonight. She's almost as bad as me when not allowed to do whatever she wants. I must remain as covert as possible. Staying in the car crosses my mind; I figure I can at least see her come and go easily, but then I notice someone carrying a guitar case around back. There must be another entrance.

Patrons slowly trickle through the front door, coming and going in waves. I wait until a sizable group collects near the door, then make my move, striding up just behind them like a chaperone, which is what I look like. The kids (they look like kids to me even though they're probably in their mid-twenties) are dressed in ripped jeans and shirts, gauges big enough to fit a fist through, and then there's me: mom of one, driver of a crossover SUV, wearer of jean capris that went out of style before I even bought them twenty years ago. The doorman doesn't even blink, bless him. He must see the mom type more than I expect. The cover is ten bucks. He swipes my card through a little square on his phone and, just like that, I'm inside.

Think dive bar with a stage and you have the Rat House. (*Rat use*, according to the burned-out neon). Every barstool is shredded from years of abuse, and the bartender looks about sixty and exhausted. At first, I can't find Lola, and panic strikes every nerve in my body before I spot her coming out of the bathroom. She is positively the most beautiful creature in the room. Her eyes are still focused and bright, so she isn't high. Yet.

Just as I thought, Emily's dad is nowhere to be seen.

Taking the nearest stool, I signal the bartender and curl my hands over my mouth, as if this shields the rest of me from my daughter. Lucky for me, she's an arrogant thing–probably riding the thrill of her successful lie. Doesn't even see her mother skulking by the bar.

"Who you stalking?" the bartender asks. The audience is becoming impatient, so the bartender is almost yelling over the racket.

"My daughter." There is no reason to lie.

He shrugs in a way suggesting this answer is reasonable enough, demanding no further explanation. "What can I get you?"

"Vodka soda. I don't give a shit if it's well."

"You think I serve much else?" He doesn't wait around for my response.

The order sits strangely on my tongue. I haven't had a drink since my disaster of a wedding. I wanted to elope, but Jimothy wouldn't have it. Or, really, his mother wouldn't. Jimothy told me that Marilyn insisted on "being there for him," but I know better. Whatever shortcomings I've ever ascribed to this woman, being stupid has never been one of them. For her, an elopement would have been cataclysmic; my triumph over the will of her favorite son. She wanted a wedding, and she got one. She paid for the entire backyard affair–the caterer, the DJ, and little Lola's fancy dress–a frilly pink thing that even my girly six-year-old hated. She refused to wear it when she saw it, but children are malleable and easily swayed by promises of a new family.

I let her do it, my future mother-in-law, mostly because I was broke. All I cared about was the ink on the marriage certificate. I'd have worn the pink dress myself if it had made Marilyn happy, but Mother Dear didn't care to include me in her wedding plans. I bought my own dress, charged it to the crush of debt her family was about to inherit. It didn't matter. The dress, like the bride, was an afterthought.

Our wedding officiant was the pastor of Marilyn's best friend's church. A significant savings, she boasted, a gift to her beloved son. The folding chair pews were taken up mostly by Jimothy's family: both his brothers, and two sets of grandparents. My side sat conspicuously bare–two co-workers whose names I've forgotten and my molly dealer who had tattooed lightning bolts in place of her eyebrows. Her name was Amber. I didn't even bother inviting my other friends, the people I did drugs with at the clubs. Most of them wouldn't have come; family, children, and clean clothes weren't exactly their cup of tea.

When Jimothy's family glanced at the opposing side, I could practically see them holding their noses. They looked like stockbrokers posting pictures of themselves handing singles to the homeless. *How lucky Regina is to have James. Her being such an orphaned wretch.*

After the ceremony, Jimothy wandered over to the bar set-up at the edge of the patio with his brothers. Time for shots. The ink was wet, but official. We were married. I sipped a glass of rosé as I watched Lola hop out of step to the Electric Slide. Suddenly, I felt Marilyn's hot breath on my neck. My new mother-in-law. Just "mother," now.

"It's a shame your mother isn't here to see her daughter get married," she said. I remember the lipstick stains on the rim of her cosmo, a deep, offensive violet that didn't match her skin tone.

Locking eyes, I said, "Would you have demanded a DNA test from her, too?"

And, in the split-second moment of defenseless fury, Marilyn shot back, "Not necessary. I can't imagine there'd have been any doubt of *your* lineage."

She'd never been more right in her life, no matter how accidentally. If my mother had been alive, she'd most certainly have arrived to this little ceremony in the same, red-bottomed hooves as her only daughter.

Marilyn hated me, but loved her son enough to hide it. She knew Lola was not her biological granddaughter. Mothers just know, I guess. She insisted on a DNA test before the wedding, which Jimothy flatly refused to consider. Even as his family told her to knock it off and let her son think whatever he wanted, Marilyn persisted. Jimothy, too, probably knew chances were low he was actually Lola's bio dad. In the years between her birth and our reunification, I'd never once contacted him. Never asked for money. When we linked up again, I'd explained my lack of communication with false stories of deep-rooted shame, grief over my mother's death, and a fierce independence gripped me like a chokehold no matter how badly I needed help. I'm certain Jimothy never believed any of those fictions completely, but I was his damsel, Lola his princess, and he'd smother his mother with a pillow before allowing either of us to slip through his fingers.

The wedding was one of many standoffs with Marilyn. After all the accusations and arguments, after I'd won, it might have been the only moment in my relationship with Marilyn where we understood one another perfectly. Her sharp distrust felt like crystallized venom, lancing the distaste puckering my mouth. A grin oozed onto my face because she was right. I was a bad woman and my baby was a cuckoo's egg and we did not belong in Marilyn's perfect little family.

I revoked the modicum of respect I felt for my mother-in-law's wrath not thirty minutes later when I caught her rage-puking in the hall bathroom. She heaved, sobbing loudly to Jimothy to get an annulment as her cheek melted against the porcelain bowl.

The following morning, I announced my decision to quit drinking. My abstinence from alcohol has been a triumphant reminder of Marilyn's shame and our mutual loathing ever since.

But she's dying now, and vodka soda has never sounded so sweet. The fizzy, clear liquid is down my throat mere seconds after the glass hits the bar. I've got years of sobriety to make up for. And, goddamn, does it hit like fireworks. The gasoline heat of pure liquor brings tears to my eyes. An instant buzz blooms in my frontal lobe, and I feel amazing. I could hurl a barstool. I could scream. I fucking missed this so much.

My pleasure dies the second my phone buzzes in my back pocket. I'm transported to the feeling of being a teenager myself, ducking phone calls from home because I'm out partying when I'm supposed to be at study group.

Silencing the call, I text Jimothy back. "Can't talk. Arguing with your daughter. Will call later."

It's not a complete lie. I know this evening isn't going to end well. Call it motherly prescience. An instinct for conflict.

Across the small room, Lola turns my way and I avoid the urge to duck. She's sitting next to Emily and some other girl I don't know, probably that other one she mentioned in the kitchen. It's stunning how acutely I repel pertinent information. My daughter stares right at me but doesn't notice me at all. She scans the room, obviously searching for someone other than her mother and her expression flags a little when she doesn't find them.

A mishmash of chairs line the space in aisles, leaving no room to move, dance, or do anything. The people are packing in with a quickness. My second soda is set on the counter, and the bartender disappears once more into the bazaar of shouted drink orders. The show must be getting ready to start.

I can only see the occasional flicker of Lola's skull from where I sit, which is enough. Maybe she just wanted to come to a show with her friends. Maybe it will be fine, and I can duck out before she heads home. I can already see myself pretending to be watching Frasier when she walks through the door, and I can be the cool mom because we finally have a secret from her dad. Maybe I was being dramatic before.

But then the band struts to the stage. Their bodies are lean in the way of teenagers but with the facial hair of young men. Each of the four has his own flair for dress that both perplexes and impresses me–ripped shirts, neon, nose-rings connected to their ears by black chains.

The lights fade abruptly, and I spot the bartender turning a dimmer switch behind the bar. It's awkward, a sudden darkness. No finesse at all.

By now, my glass is empty and I'm fingering some ice out of habit. For a minute, I'm wishing I had another drink, and then the music starts, and I forget all about alcohol.

The music is terrible. Just garbage. It's so bad it's offensive. The off-key lead singer croons to the back of the bar, terrified to make eye contact with anyone in the crowd. It's some kind of ska shit but worse, because ska was never all that good anyway, and the drummer can't seem to lay a reliable beat, so the rest just sounds like a discordant mess. I wish I could stab a drink umbrella through each of my eardrums to make it stop.

This is Beefy Reefer. And the girls–Lola, too–are eating it up.

The bartender edges in my direction and I flag him down.

He gestures to my empty glass, which I cover with my hand while shaking my head. I have other things to discuss.

"These guys fucking suck!" I say, and assume his small smile means he heard me, and agrees. And I feel good about that. They *do* suck, and I should know. I may be a vanilla, middle-aged mom, but I do know music. Taste doesn't go away just because you move to the suburbs. I'd wager a person needs good songs even more once the kids come. A parent can only listen to so many hours of the Twiddle Bops or whatever the fuck little kids watch nowadays before wanting to blow their brains out.

So I'm feeling good, superior even, when I turn back. My eyes fall on my kid, and then the drummer, and then my kid again and I see it. The look. The admiration.

These two have met before, my beautiful child and this motherfucker who has a full beard and pit sweat. She is seventeen years old. He bangs on the toms like a second grader who's proud of himself for being in the advanced drumming class with the big kids. He sucks at music, at being a man, at everything and he wants my daughter. If I was a stronger woman, my glass would have shattered in my hands.

The set eventually finishes (to the delight of everyone in the audience with taste), and while a few little groupies linger behind, the Rat House clears out with alarming swiftness, leaving only a handful of people among whom to hide myself from view. I feel confident that if Jimothy was here he would want me to intervene–well, if he was here, Lola would never have been able to come, but if he'd seen the way this drummer gawked at his daughter, he'd be right on board with an intervention.

As I plan my move, Lola is distracted. She's too giddy to bother glancing at the bar and nervously toys with her bead bracelet, awaiting her paramour's return. Emily and the other girl have disappeared.

"Goddamn," I say as I gesture toward the empty bar. "Is it always like this?"

He nods. "Why do you think I even invite such shit to play here? It brings crowds. Terrible crowds, but terrible crowds still buy booze."

"Have you tried hiring actual musicians?"

"Funny thing about talented artists—they avoid clubs called the Rat House like the plague. And they certainly don't play for a fee."

"You must love trash. Why else would you be here? This place is a hole."

Thankfully, he laughs. "I inherited the building from my grandfather. It was a speakeasy back in the day. I got a plaque in the back I've never bothered to put up. Believe it or not, this place is considered a historic building, approved by the city. Can't ever be demolished, no matter how much of a piece of shit it becomes."

"Why call it the Rat House? 'Speakeasy' has a better sound to it."

He shrugs. I'm not sure if it's because he doesn't know or doesn't want to speak the reason aloud, but I no longer care. Mr. Drummer Boy descends from the small stage and beelines towards my Lola.

The pair doesn't hesitate to slip out of sight, which is precisely when I cease to function like a typical, rational adult and mutate into a primitive animal protecting its young. A surge of adrenaline-spiked blood blots away all noise, and I'm guided solely by the thrum of my heart, which threatens to punch its way through my ribcage. I can feel everything, down to my fingernails. A mosquito couldn't slip past me in this state. This fucker doesn't stand a chance.

I am deaf to the bartender shouting at me that I can't go back there, or even the surprised proclamation from Emily, who sees me turning the corner and shouts, "Lola's mom!" Everything happening outside my body is both inconsequential yet sticky. My psyche is focused on Lola, rejecting everything outside my instinct to protect her.

I follow a scent–I swear I can smell her with him. I follow my nose through the backstage area. The club's rear exit door squeaks heavily as it slams shut behind me. The two are surrounded by piles of dark back alley trash and haloed by a streetlight that cascades jaundiced yellow onto Lola's otherwise vibrant features.

A twenty-something is squeezing my teenager's ass. She's smiling. He's whispering to her conspiratorially, too low for me to work out. I feel my heartbeat in my fingertips. My ears burn hot. There's a broken mop leaning against the building. I grab it.

"Get in the fucking car, Lola," I say.

Finally, she sees me. Rapid-fire emotions break across her face. Her expression careens from shock to terror, then settles on unmitigated fury.

"Mom! What are you doing here?"

The drummer releases her like a lit stick of dynamite and steps back.

"Get into the fucking car. I won't say it again."

The rage in my kid's eyes is evident. She is pissed, but she is smart enough to recognize when she is outmatched. Maybe it's a feral thing, some remnant of our wild ancestors. She will argue with me, oh yes, she will. Might even hate me. But she won't unleash her anger now.

The drummer continues to back away, tripping over a trash can in the dark. Lola eyes the mop in my hand, smirks, and steps toward her secret boyfriend. She takes his hand. It's an act of resistance. The performance electrifies every hair on my body, and my vision constricts. All I can see is this man uselessly holding her back. I launch the broom at his head. It misses.

"Mom!" Lola shouts.

Words sputter out of me. "Car. Now."

Sensing her defeat, Lola shoulder-checks me on her way toward the parking lot, but I don't move an inch. As soon as she is safely away, I square off with this man, lunging toward him before he can collect himself. He trips over his own feet and lands on his ass.

"How old is that girl?" I ask.

"Look, we didn't do anything, I swear. She said she was eighteen, I *swear*!"

"I don't care what she said. How did you meet her?"

"At a show! She was in the audience! Nothing happened."

"You know Emily?"

Even in the dark, the thud of realization freezing his features is apparent. He's stuck, and he knows it.

"Emily is sixteen. They're in high school. Even if they were eighteen, and you fucking *know* they're not, it's still pathetic. What are you? Thirty?"

"No!"

He tries to stand but I push him back to the ground. I can feel my teeth sharpening into fangs.

"Give me your license."

He finds the slightest bit of courage and tells me to go fuck myself. What a gentleman.

I grab his stupid shirt collar, twist it so that the fabric hugs his neck like a noose, and repeat my demand. "Or else we can call the goddamn cops. Pick your poison."

"I won't talk to her anymore. Just get the fuck off me."

My patience is gone and all I see is a punchable face in a dark alley with no witnesses. Upon reflection, I can only assume the adrenaline pique that came over me was like those urban legends of mothers lifting cars off their kids. I was immovable and unstoppable. I could hurl a car, if there'd been one within reach. The intensity of my stare dries my eyes to cotton, but I don't blink. I don't think I've blinked once since I spotted the guy, afraid that if I do, he'd slither out of my grasp before I am done with him. My pupils must be tight as pins.

So the drummer complies. He hands over his driver's license.

Releasing him, I try to read his date of birth but it's too dark. I have to use the flashlight on my phone to see, which really sucks the wind from a person's sails when they're trying to be a hardass. Having his license isn't proof of anything, but he's frightened enough to not be thinking clearly. Or else I'm mad enough to have properly put the fear of God into him.

The drummer is getting ready to make a break for it when I finally find the digits of his birth year. Am I yelling? My throat aches. "Twenty-eight. Fuck me. You are a fucking pervert. Come anywhere near my daughter again, and I'll find you in your bed and slit your throat."

"You're fucking insane."

"No shit! Stay away from Lola. Stay away from all those teenagers. You're a grown man. Find yourself a grown woman, if you can find one stupid enough to fuck you."

This snaps him out of his fear, catapulting him into offended rage. "Fuck you, bitch! Give me my license." He postures as if he's suddenly remembered that he's a man and I'm not. He could clock me if he felt like it.

But I refuse to give him any satisfaction. In a split second, I know what to do. The compulsion slams into me, and placing the license between my teeth, I crack my jaw with my fist. My mandible joints pop, nerves aflame with warning. Oh, it's beautiful. My mouth lolls open, dislocated and tongue stretched too long. Sharp pain spiders into my temples.

Before the drummer can react, his license is hurtling into my throat. I swallow the thing, wincing as it sticks and grinds along my esophagus, all the way down to my stomach. My muscles move slowly, but I don't allow discomfort to show on my face, even as the rectangle of plastic wages war on my insides.

The drummer is speechless, mouth agape. I smile, lean real close to his face, and whisper, "I'll mail it back to you once I finally shit it out."

He doesn't say anything else, just runs. I watch him flee, grinning with my unhinged jaw the few times he glances back to see if I'm still watching. Of course I am watching—I won't move until he is thoroughly out of sight. I want the last thing he remembers from our encounter to be my satisfied leer, illuminated by that grungy streetlight.

I want him to see me every time he closes his eyes. At least for a while.

Then, once I'm sure the drummer is long gone, I bend my knees, clutching my chest. His license is stuck near my sternum. I want to rip myself open and tear the foreign invader from my body, and my body dutifully does the job for me. I vomit everything onto the pavement–his license, blood, and foam. I like the look of this dipshit's mugshot covered in my puke, so I make sure to fish the plastic card from the puddle of puke. After popping my jaw back into place, I stow the license in my purse and march to my car, jean capris dotted with bile.

My euphoria is promptly squashed by the visage of my daughter. She is not grateful to be rescued from statutory rape. Instead, she is grimacing herself into another dimension from the front passenger seat of the Kia. I square my shoulders and don't break eye contact with her. She can't know this experience shook me. And I've got to consider things from her point of view. I can remember the freedom of blooming adulthood, the adrenaline rush of feeling like the most beautiful creature in the room, only to have it crushed under my mother's envious boot. Lola didn't do anything out of the ordinary for a kid her age. Shit, I did much, much worse. Making out with a talentless wannabe is innocent playground shenanigans compared to the things I got up to at seventeen. At least she wasn't sucking on a pacifier until the E wore off or coming home at dawn wearing someone else's clothes.

I don't even open my car door before she starts screaming at me.

"I can't believe you! Why would you do this? What is wrong with you?"

All fair points—if I was the one making them. My previous sense of loving protectiveness is sucked out of me immediately. A tension headache squeezes my skull. Putting the car in drive, I tighten my white knuckles on the steering wheel and fire back. "God damn it, Lola! What the fuck is wrong with *you*? He's twenty-eight years old. Twenty-eight! And his band fucking *sucks*!"

"His band? That's what you're mad about?"

"Of course that's not it, but it doesn't help. You lied to me to meet up with some guy and that's the one you pick? Fuck me, kid, I thought I raised you with better taste."

At this, she's quiet, but only for a moment. "Are you kidding me, Mom?"

"No, I'm not kidding you. He's a loser, and a wretched musician. He can't score with women his own age. Have some self-respect, Lola. Christ."

"You're saying this man, like, groomed me or something and you're mad at *me*? That's some demented victim-blaming bullshit." She's got her arms crossed, eyes welling up with tears as she points her gaze anywhere but toward me.

The red light at the intersection sneaks up on me, and I slam the brakes so hard she braces herself against the dash. "Stop the poor-me schtick. It's beneath you. Besides, I've already dealt with that pervert."

This nabs her attention. "What did you do?"

"That's none of your business."

"It is my business! He's my boyfriend!"

A cackle explodes from my mouth with the decibels and power to crack the windshield. "Like hell he is."

She flops into her seat, dejected and crying. "I hate you."

"Join the club."

We mean it, too. Both of us. I don't think there is much worse we can say to one another, until I blurt my thoughts into the quiet of the car. "This is why we need your father."

She doesn't respond, only turns her back to me, trembling with quiet sobs.

Chapter 4

My bathroom mirror reflects a ghastly image: blood smears around my lips and fingertips, eyes weighed down by dark bags. My hair is a frizzy crown of salty brunette. My throat stings like a dozen paper cuts with every breath. I can't be sure if Lola noticed my bloodied condition, since she sprinted into the house before the car was even in park. Part of me hopes she didn't. A more malignant part of me hopes she did.

Jimothy should be up my ass by now, wanting to talk, worried about whatever spat Lola and I found ourselves in. My husband is a compulsive problem solver, and we two are his greatest challenge–his Everest, you might say. I can't imagine him not intervening after my curt text, but he hasn't. My phone remains eerily silent, which leads me to wonder if Lola got to him before I did.

I hate myself for thinking this way about my daughter. I used to think that I was jealous of their easy father-daughter affection, and I couldn't understand why that might be. She is my daughter, not a competing female in the herd. I now know it isn't jealousy which causes this uneasiness, but suspicion mixed with shame. I'll never not be suspicious of every person in my orbit, even her. I was raised by a mother who distrusted everyone, even me. As Lola ages, she becomes more articulate about my failings, and there are plenty. I'm a bad mother. The proof is written all over my face. Just look at me now.

Another person would feel bad about what I've just done. Horrified. Aghast, even. But I don't. I even sort of admire how I look like a barfight in capri pants. I rotate the drummer's license between my fingers. Its plastic sheath is now dappled with bile-thinned blood, giving it an air of modern watercolor art. His name is Calvin Lehr.

My stomach humbles me before I can get too cocky. It happens from time to time when I start eating things I shouldn't, but even as my insides throb from the night's abuse, the vision of the drummer as he flees puts a pep in my step. I feel light and untouchable. For the first time in ages, I feel firmly in control.

And I quite like it.

✿ ✿ ✿

Lola does not emerge from her room for most of the following day. All Saturday, I drink warm broth and try to concentrate on Jimothy and his sick mother and how my daughter is still too young to make good choices, but too old to accept direction. I think about all this despite my better judgement, until the daylight wanes and my body signals its desire for solid food with crippling stomach cramps. Lola has yet to make a single sound.

My 6 p.m. knock on her door is greeted with silent hostility. Must be a motherly sixth sense. I know she is listening and I know she hears me when I call to her, when

I question whether she's hungry and wants some mac and cheese (her favorite food). I know she hears every word.

I text my husband, inquiring about his mother so that he might become distracted enough to not ask about our goings on at home.

"She's sleeping," he says. "I'm talking to a real estate agent about selling her house. The equity should fund a decade of assisted living."

He stops there, but I imagine the end of that sentence. *If she lives that long.*

Evening fades into night, and before I know it, Saturday has melted into Sunday, Sunday into Monday, and another work week is upon me. Lola leaves for school before I even wake for work, slamming the door hard enough to vibrate a family photo off the wall. My insistence on buying cheap plastic frames pays off because it doesn't break.

I'm too irritated to create a morning drive playlist, so I defer to my most repeated list and start my Kia. I don't know why, but this particular morning a song I've listened to thousands of times jumps out at me, almost as if this was the first time I've ever listened to it. This happens very rarely, mainly because I repeat favorite songs to death. My track-repeating habit is so obsessive that, after a few months, I'd rather eat my own finger than hear a favorite song again. My need to find something to obsess over keeps me on a continual hunt for new music, something fresh to raise my pulse and bathe my brain in whichever chemical is released when humans listen to good music. It's like an addiction, and like most addictions the same old shit just doesn't cut it after a while. So, to have a song reach out from retirement and grab me anew is something special, and while idling at a long light I can't stop myself from imagining it as an opener to a kickass set. The right lights, right set up, and it could be spectacular. Not like Beefy Reefer and their garbage. I could really draw a crowd, given the chance.

Reality strangles the life out of my idea before it ever takes off, though. The drive to work is too short, as always. The parking lot is full, as always. I park in the alley behind the building, enter through the front double doors, sit at my desk and am greeted by an internal message from Cassandra the second my computer boots up.

Meeting in ten. Where are you?

She sent it twenty minutes ago. I, of course, ignored the memo she'd provided last week. I'm fifteen minutes late by the time I log into the video call. I catch Cassandra's masked smirk of delight as my name populates the list of attendees.

"Look who's finally decided to join us?" she says, interrupting our accountant mid-sentence.

"Sorry, all!" I say.

Cassandra pauses, hoping beyond hope that I offer some sort of excuse for her to pick apart, and when I don't, she prompts the accountant to continue. Thankfully, I love pointless meetings–there's no better way to pass the time at work than to daydream about my drive home with my camera off.

From what I can gather, the purpose of this virtual meeting is to give Cassandra the company's undivided attention. She speaks three times more than anyone else, and the information given is beat-for-beat the same information discoverable in our quarterly reporting, which is sent from each department via email. I don't even realize it's over until I look down and see a black screen that reads *the host has ended the meeting*. Good. If anyone needs anything from me they can email like a regular goddamn person.

I imagine Cassandra will be gossiping about my lack of enthusiasm, which is the main reason she grinds my gears so fiercely. She's like a gnat with a sense of entitlement. A gnat with purpose. A gnat who loves its place in the world. How can a gnat be so unrepentantly self-satisfied? The idea of her contentment makes me want to break things.

My phone vibrates in my pocket, and I loathe to check it fearing it's another lecture from Cassandra, but once I do, my stomach drops. It's my husband. I have two voicemails and four unread texts. It takes a few seconds to process his question, but once I do, all the skin on my body flushes as if on fire.

Why isn't Lola at school?

That little *shit*.

Lola has not exactly ratted me out to her dad. She ditched school knowing he'd get the automatic text the school sends for every absence. She's probably expecting a furious call from me right now, but I'm not going to give her the satisfaction of playing into her little game. If she wants to fuck up her attendance record in the name of passive-aggression, she can be my guest.

Not feeling well. I might have let her stay up too late last night. I'll call the school.

I soothe my guilt by repeating to myself that Jimothy doesn't need any extra stress right now. I'll have this all resolved by the time he gets home, anyway. Lola will understand her place by the time I'm through with her. I'll show her who her mother really is and dare her to challenge me ever again.

Either that, or one of us will be dead. In any case, the problem will be solved.

After lunch I call in sick, hoping to beat Lola to the house, but she is already home and sleeping by the time I get home. She likely waited until I left for work before retreating straight back to her room. Chances are, her phone is on silent, too.

The drummer's license is hidden in my sock drawer, but I want to look at him again in a better light. I desperately want to see what my daughter sees in him, why she would choose such a person to risk the trouble in which she will now find herself. I want to see him because I know, deep in my gut, that he is exactly the type of man-child I might have dated at her age. Out of some sick compulsion, I grab my phone and google "Beefy Reefer." Nothing really comes up aside from a few pictures of the band playing at the Rat House. The bartender looms in the background of each photo looking as resigned as ever and I feel sorry for the guy, having to funnel his birthright into the gullets of ungrateful young people and sad, old drunks, but we've all got problems.

I scroll and click, getting nowhere. The urge to slam a door overcomes me with ferociousness. I need to get out of my house. Why am I waiting for a teenager to grace me with her presence? Let her mope on her own. If Lola refuses to speak to me, and Jimothy hasn't tried calling, I'm off the hook. Radio silence can only mean they are more overwhelmed than I am.

The Rat House is closed at this time of day, its parking lot decorated with burger wrappers and old shopping bags. Trash blows across the black terrain, catching on the exposed rebar of crumbling parking blocks. A crow announces my arrival with a croak and flies away. Even from the outside, the building smells of vomit, and I wonder how much of it is mine as I cram a handwritten note through the security bars for the front door, hoping the bartender will take me up on what I'm offering. We both could use a fresh start.

Chapter 5

I'm not sure what I expected when leaving an unsigned note at a bar reading, "Your acts suck. Call me!" but radio silence wasn't it. A note of such nature would have *me* rush to pick up the phone, if only to scold the sender for their audacity. The bartender, it seems, does not possess the same ultra-high levels of indignance as I do, so two days later I am once again traveling the familiar streets leading to the Rat House.

Tonight is a regular bar night, no live events, and the regulars sit scattershot within the small space, no one daring near proximity to another for fear of accidental eye contact. The bartender doesn't miss a beat, setting a shot glass in front of an empty seat and pouring a round of clear liquid from an unmarked bottle. Not vodka, this time—mystery hooch.

"I got your note," he says.

Accepting his offering, I force a straight face as alcoholic ooze stings the mutilated flesh of my throat. "And you didn't call."

"You know," he refills the glass. "I had the strangest conversation with that drummer boy after the show."

I drink again, smaller sips this time. "What does that little chickenshit have to say for himself?"

"Nothing about himself, but he said the craziest shit about you."

"I bet he did. He was so easy to scare, it wasn't even fun."

The bartender doesn't appear fazed. "That's twenty dollars for the two of them," he says, pointing to my empty glass. "Now, why don't you tell me what you had in mind?"

Well. The thing is, I have very little in mind. I want to play music, and I want my husband to come home, and I want to have a healthy, bonded relationship with my kid. I haven't planned much else, even as I drove here with the exact intent of speaking to this man about what I want to do. A man whose name I don't even know.

"What's your name, anyway?" I ask.

"Hank," he says.

"I'm going to be honest with you, Hank. I didn't really think this far ahead."

"Then what made you drop that note?"

I lean back in the barstool and think about it. The drink is already getting to me. It is only my second time drinking in eleven years. It's been a long, hard eleven years without liquor and I've missed it more than I realized.

"I don't know. Honestly, I think I'm over being in my forties. My life is boring, and I want to do something thrilling that doesn't involve spying on my teenage daughter. She hates me right now, by the way."

"Hating your mother is a rite of passage for a lot of kids."

"Sure. I was an awful child to my mother, but even then, Mom was always the first person I'd call when I needed anything. Lola seems to find me repulsive in every aspect. I guess that could be normal, but it doesn't feel normal."

The way Hank stares makes me change tack. "Music is infectious when well done. It's an escape. I figure, seeing the shit out there calling themselves a band, I might as well give it a shot."

"You play an instrument or something?"

"Not a single one." The liquor is bitter, but it's not the reason I wince. I sound like such an asshole.

"So, you plan to get on stage and lecture everyone about their bad taste?"

The thought worms its way into my brain, and just like that, I've got it.

"No, no. I plan to show them how to do it right."

Hank is not entirely convinced of my idea by the time I leave the bar, but he doesn't say no. He warns me that every DJ he's brought into the Rat House has never returned. Not the kind of crowd that likes to move a lot, he says. Still, this doesn't dissuade me. The pieces keep slotting together so perfectly that by the time I'm in my driveway, I've got the first half of a setlist constructed. I know exactly what I'm going to do. I just need to figure out how to do it.

Lola is sitting at the kitchen table when I return, greeting me with the same blank expression her father does when he has something important to discuss. I make for the fridge without a word. Nothing worth cooking. I rifle through the cabinets, looking for something to prepare for dinner. The tension between Lola and me carries me like the tide, unmooring me so that I run into a cabinet door I'd forgotten to close. I'm holding a sack of flour and a can of baked beans, considering what to do with them, when Lola breaks the silence.

"Grandma isn't doing well, I guess."

"I know," I say, setting the beans on the counter. This isn't what I expected.

"I never really got to know her." She stares absently, anxiously twisting a ring around her middle finger.

I am suddenly overcome with unexplainable rage. My mother-in-law tortured Jimothy over Lola's parentage for years. *I* might have deserved her ire, but he and a little child did not. Marilyn is a rotten piece of shit. Yet somehow, she managed to raise the most compassionate human on the planet, as if nature knew she needed a kid like Jimothy to balance out her horribleness. Who else would bother to care for her? And now, because of *that woman*, I am alone with my child, who is seriously facing the concept of death for the first time.

I want to say, "That raggedy bitch is a God-tier narcissist, and I might respect her hustle if I didn't hate her so goddamn much." Instead, I rein in my temper and do my best. "I'd say you aren't missing much. That woman is vile, but I know that is little consolation."

"Dad says she's going to die soon." Lola looks up at me, her eyes so big and brown, and my heart breaks.

I should comfort her, wrap her up in my arms and tell her it's okay to feel sad when people die (because it is, because even if a person is horrible, their death still jolts the system like defibrillation paddles to the chest). Yet, instead I slap my hands to the counter and ask, "Why the sudden sympathy for a woman you don't even know?"

But Lola doesn't go on the attack like I expect. Instead, she begins to cry. "I'm sorry, Mom. I'm sorry I lied to you."

The can of beans crashes to the floor as I glide toward my child. There are so many things I want to do in the moment, things a good mom would do, like hold her and stroke her hair. I want to tell her I'm sorry for being such a freak of a person and promise to do better if she promises to let me in when she needs me.

Instead, all I say is, "Your Dad will be home real soon."

I pull her close. She nods against my chest, and we stay this way for what seems like an hour because it's been so long since our last true embrace. I miss my daughter, and I miss the person I used to be when raising her.

When we finally separate, we both chuckle, wiping our eyes with our sleeves. We make instant ramen for dinner. I pour the broth out of her bowl like used to when she was little, and she doesn't complain when I hand it to her, correcting me only once she finishes eating.

"The broth isn't so bad, you know."

"I should have asked. Force of habit, I guess."

But she shrugs and says she likes it both ways, and I think, climbing into bed many hours later, surfing a surge of sweet memories and new futures, that I was right all along.

The world really is better off when bad people die.

Chapter 6

This resurgence of positive vibes between me and Lola stifles my longing for adventure, and for a while I forget all about the Rat House and setlists. Work plods along, Lola aces her calculus test, and Jimothy reports a lull in his mother's cliff-dive into senility. He found a great place for her and has a few interested buyers for her house. Looks like he might make it home before the month's end. We speak on the phone every night, and he even notices a new lilt in Lola's tone. She seems lighter, he says.

"I knew you two would find your groove!" His statement is emphasized with silent applause, which sours me in an instant because while his words appear benign, I manipulate the sentiment behind them.

Thank God you haven't ruined the family in my absence.

It's a deliberate misinterpretation, and it's unfair to poor Jimothy. I'm being dramatic, so I decide to let it go. "Yeah, it's been rather nice around here lately."

"That's good." His words float through the phone and disappear as if he's thinking of something else before he's even finished his sentence. There is a cry in the background, sounding more frustrated than sorrowful, and he swiftly ends the call. I feel bad for him, I do, but part of me is glad he is gone for a little while longer, and I didn't expect to feel this way.

Lola bangs around in the kitchen and I join her, setting my Bluetooth speaker on the counter. It's spaghetti night, so I find my Sinatra playlist and keep the volume low. Lola hates lounge singers, but today she doesn't comment on my selection.

"Do you have a playlist for everything?" she asks, salting the water.

"Don't you?"

She shrugs. "Isn't it cliché to play Sinatra every time we have spaghetti?"

"What do you have against Sinatra?"

"I don't know. It's old-people music."

The cold from the package of ground beef in my hands stings my fingers, so I set it down while searching for the garlic salt. "It was old-people music when I was young, too."

"Do you even like it? Or are you just used to it?"

The question stops me. "You know, that's a good question. It might be a little of both."

Lola points to the speaker. She wants to pick a new song, and the idea delights me.

As I fumble about with the meatballs (Jimothy usually handles this part), the speaker rapid-fire clicks as Lola skims through our monstrous digital collection of music. Sometimes I skim through her selections, generally bemused if not annoyed by her choices. But tonight, she's taken great care to find just the right song. It begins low and slow, a delicate synth melody I'm expecting to surge into some pseudo-powerful EDM, but it never does. Instead, it ebbs like a wave, retreating to a soothing lull just when you'd expect an explosion. I find myself pausing my cooking to listen, enjoying the slightly off-kilter feeling I get. I'm charmed by how well its structure eludes me.

"Who is this?" I ask.

"They're called False Fingers. I listen to them when I can't sleep."

It sounds entirely unlike her usual fare. "How did you find an act like them?"

"Friends," she says, blushing at once and turning away from me.

She means Calvin, but I don't comment any further. "Text me the band's name so I don't forget."

We share music most of the night, swapping songs and making faces, nodding on occasion when we approve. Lola pulls her lips toward her teeth when she doesn't like something, just like Jimothy, but she sits with her right leg tucked under her left just like me. I used to marvel at her all the time when she was little, piecing her together with bits of me and bits of her father, a puzzle to solve. But kids grow and evolve beyond the shadow of their genetics. They become something else, something new and wholly unique. Maybe that's why parents fight with their teenagers so fiercely–they just don't recognize them anymore. It's a recipe for an existential crisis as their contributed ingredients become a soup they never agreed to make. That's been my issue with Lola, but watching her now as the night falls, I still see so much of myself reflecting back.

I'm sure that doesn't help our interactions, because I am an asshole. Assholes clash with other assholes, each party rebuking the mirror being held in front of their faces. This fact alone explains so much of our relationship.

❂ ❂ ❂

It's past midnight when I startle awake to the sound of rummaging in the medicine cabinet.

"Where's the Benadryl?" she asks.

"Do you have hives again?" Lola breaks out in hives without explanation and with startling frequency.

"I can't sleep."

Allergy medicine has the same drowsy effect on me, which is how I know the bottle is on my bathroom counter. "It's in my room. Go ahead and grab it."

From my bed, I can hear Lola opening and closing drawers in my bathroom. I must have knocked the bottle into a drawer in a sloppy attempt at cleaning. I'm not suspicious, not thinking anything of why she's been in there for longer than it should take to grab the medicine. I should have known better. There is a reason I usually don't let Lola rummage unaccompanied in my room.

"What is this?" She's stomping down the hallway with an intensity that raises the hairs on my neck. "How did you get this, Mom?"

Ice-cold dread pools in my gut seconds before I understand what she's talking about–the sheen of the laminate under the low light gives it away. She's found the drummer's license. The implications of her discovery send my brain into a tailspin searching for explanations.

"Get what?" I ask, hoping I'm wrong while knowing I'm not.

"Calvin told me you took this. He said you...was he right? What did you do?"

Now I'm standing, fists perched indignantly on my hips. "I knew he was lying about his age. I told him I'd call the cops unless he handed it over. Little chickenshit is almost thirty, Lola."

Her eyes narrow with knowing. He must have told her everything, but I've been a liar longer than that idiot Calvin has been alive.

The quickest way to make grotesque accusations cease is to make the accusing party speak them aloud. If they're horrified enough, they won't dare, and you can feign ignorance. I'm praying my child has enough sense to stop before she starts.

"I imagine he'd spin all sorts of stories to make him seem like less of a slimeball, so I'm immensely curious about what he's said. Tell me, Lola."

I stare back at Lola until her conviction slowly breaks down, and she bites her bottom lip to keep anything from spilling out. Her doubt flushes my veins with warm relief. Should I try to embrace her? She hands me the license before I can lift my arms.

"Nothing," she says. "He didn't say anything."

She flees to her room, and I say nothing to stop her, rubbing the license under my thumb. My blood is crusty on its edges, and I turn off the lights hoping Lola didn't look hard enough to notice.

Chapter 7

From that moment on, I keep Calvin's license in my purse. No more opportunities for Lola to find the evidence. I could throw it in the garbage, but something stops me every time I try.

Hank the bartender acts astonished when I ring him up. "I thought you'd chickened out."

"When's your next opening?"

Due to a cancellation: two weeks. Saturday. It's mine.

I spend days looking into DJ equipment, understanding with a swiftness that I have no idea what I'm doing. But the internet is plentiful, and I am an exacting student when I want to be. My DJ controller–platter? It's referred to as both–arrives overnight, and I tell Lola I'm working overtime and lock myself in my room to get comfortable with my purchases.

The set up is both more intimidating than I expected, and less. The sight of it makes me want to ring Hank up and cancel, but each time I reach for my phone to do so, my stubborn pride stops me. The software is downloaded, my headphones connected, and I have the set list planned. All the hard work is done–now all I need to do is practice.

At first glance, there are so many buttons and ways to push them that I can't get even the most basic acceleration without fucking it up. The mechanics are simple enough to understand, yet much more difficult to manage with any sort of competence. I'm banking on the patrons of the Rat House not knowing any better, or at least being forgiving to a garbage first timer. The multiple functions overwhelm me. It's like using chopsticks–there exists in my brain some kind of block preventing me from *getting* it. My fingers and my head work together only as well as bitterly divorced parents during a child exchange: the intent is there, but it takes many attempts and oversight by a judge to get the point across.

I couldn't use chopsticks for thirty years, not until we vacationed in Tokyo for our fifth wedding anniversary, and I had no choice. My table manners repulsed the staff at the ramen restaurant, but I learned. I figure that's all I need to do now. I must immerse myself in this and nothing else, foregoing all other responsibilities. Lola is keeping a healthy distance–for now, anyway. She can feed herself and drive herself to school. Jimothy is still managing the bills while away. It's perfect.

That night, I ignore Jimothy when he tries to call and don't feel bad about it. Not one bit.

✿ ✿ ✿

Things to do when creating a new persona:
- Have money
- Create a new name
- Book a venue
- Have money

- Think of the ambiance—do I need a fog machine?
- Have money
- Costume—no one needs to see my face
- Have money
- Have money
- Money
- $$

Turns out that having money is a real game changer, and while Jimothy makes a solid wage working in tech, we don't have the kind of fuck-you money necessary to realize my ambitions. Looks like I'm going to have to rely on homegrown charm to sell my image, which means I'm fucked.

I want Coachella-style lights. Smoke machines. There's a song I'd like to use in my set that uses audio clips from a zombie movie as the chorus, and I envision sexy, topless zombie babes spinning on poles next to me on stage. This is the type of shit that makes a memorable show. In lieu of big-tittied dancers, I'll have to do my best to sound marginally competent.

I've spent the past week fiddling with every button, every setting, smoothing my transitions, understanding how to splice this in where, remove this how. I'm getting better. It's amazing how quickly a person can learn a new hobby when they don't care about paying bills or being fired. I can see the blade of the guillotine creeping ever closer to my neck with every snarky reply I send to Cassandra, so I can only assume my termination is imminent. I just don't care. Instead, I digest one thousand milligrams of caffeine per day, fingers trembling as I coast on the bare minimum at work and let Lola scavenge for herself.

By now, my debut is in three days and sleep eludes me with fiercer persistence each passing night–dread shakes me like a screaming baby back to consciousness every time I try. Then there's a name, my stage name, and I can't even come up with a scramble of letters. It's a crucial missing piece in my project, haunting me. Only one name sticks in my mind and I hate it immediately.

Disco Mama.

I might as well hobble on stage in a walker cushioned with tennis balls. Acts nowadays have absurd monikers like 'barfshart' or some silly bullshit written in morse code. Beefy Reefer is right on trend. Not that I'm realistically trying to compete with new bands or even attract younger crowds (as if I could!). I just want to listen to music as loud as possible with no one around to tell me to stop, and I want to choose whatever I want to hear, and I want to melt into the subwoofers until everyone's eyeballs jolt out of their sockets. I want to forget who I am and be someone else. But do I want to be Disco Mama? Really?

The sheets crinkle under my weight. My pillowcase scratches against the mattress as I pummel the flat pillow into a tighter ball under my neck. I'm sweating. I'm exhilarated.

I'm drowning in deep regret.

Mother Music. Why do all my names have a geriatric connotation? Do I really have so little else to assign to my personality?

Card Eater. No.

Just my name? No, much much worse.

Jimothy's Wife. I quite like this one. It's mysterious and slightly silly. No one will understand it. But "Jimothy" might be too ridiculous a name for the audience.

Lola would be perfect. I had an affinity for the name, long before I bestowed it upon my daughter. It's a fluid name, assertively feminine but transcending age. Your grandmother could be a Lola. So could your baby niece. So could a stripper, or your dental hygienist. One Lola could be all four of those.

My mind latches onto this theory, refusing to let go, and by sun-up I've got a mental Rolodex of all the types of people befitting each type of DJ name and absolutely zero minutes of sleep.

Then, I spend my entire day at work thinking about costumes. The thought of someone recognizing me, however slim, fills me with potent revulsion. I hate full-face masks and find them silly, but still want my mouth and eyes obscured in some way. Sunglasses would look cheap and stupid, but maybe that matches my first-time DJ energy? I fall asleep at my desk with four pairs of sun-glasses in my online cart. No one bothers to wake me up.

To an outsider I must appear to be chin-deep in a midlife crisis. Maybe I am.

✿ ✿ ✿

The day of the show arrives like a bag of oranges thrown down the stairs–a mess, unexpected and heavy. The reality of what I've signed up for bruises my confidence in a chaotic and spectacular fashion.

Lola spends the morning making it worse by reminding me about her plans with Emily. I think she thought I was toying with her when I told her to go out with her friends, have fun. She responds by interrogating me about what I'm doing that evening too, likely fearing that I intended to stalk her like I had the other weekend. Eventually, my apathy becomes clear enough for her to bound out the door without a goodbye, leaving me alone with my equipment and a countdown. Instead of sitting alone in a dark house, steeping in regret and second thoughts, I pack my stuff and head toward the Rat House, four hours early.

I park my Kia as far away from the entrance as possible, lingering with the ignition on and praying some of the people wandering by don't knock on my window, thinking I'm selling drugs. I might not look the type to sell drugs from a barren parking lot, but that's never stopped a junkie from trying. I know from experience.

I dial Hank's number in a panic, speaking before he's finished saying hello. "How soon until you get here?"

He mumbles something about listening to his gut next time but agrees to let me inside early for set up.

The stage is dusty and poorly lit. Light filters through the thin, grimy windows running the rim of the ceiling, each covered by stripes of steel bars. This whole place is wall-to-wall OSHA violations. If this all goes to hell, I might try to get it condemned–if only so I don't have to face my shame if I pass by the building in the future, the memory of my performance clinging to its vaporous existence on the dark scaffolding. It would be easier to face the Rat House's desolation than to see it alive without me, thrumming with noise and people and fun and booze. A lively bar suggests that the scene is still thriving–it's just *me* who is past their prime. But I can't think of things like this while I am setting up, can't consider the option of failure. That invites doubt and nerves which will kill me before I even get off the ground.

Backing towards the bar, I examine my stage and find myself hot with embarrassment. What a joke. It's a folding table and some disco lights I used for Jimothy's fortieth birthday party in the backyard. Some exposed wires lead to sad little speakers. The whole arrangement is crowned by my middle-aged body, cloaked in black sweats and the LED glasses I stole from Lola's room last night. Behind me, a bottle clinks and two shots are poured. Hank the bartender leaves the bottle and disappears into the back.

"Fuck," I say. The empty room echoes the sentiment. "Just...fuck."

Lights yellowed with age cast sad shadows in the crevice of my face as I waffle between glasses and no glasses. I hate everything about what I am doing, so I leave the bathroom, down two shots and then pour two more, before returning to the privacy of the single-stall women's room. I can see my reflection changing as warm confidence slowly washes across my cheeks, my sinuses stinging, eyes watering. *This* is why I love to drink. This moment right here. The rest of my night will be spent chasing the initial high of the first pour, and because I am relentless, this has historically led to me being pinned behind a toilet as I lament my choices. I figure I've got a few hours to either allow the buzz to settle or black out from excess. Let's see which part of me wins. The best part of that old bag Marilyn finally dying is that it gave me the freedom to have this moment here, booze in hand. I've missed it so much.

When I leave the bathroom the second time, the bar is brighter, but not by much. My cheeks are red. The door is wailing on rusty hinges, letting the first patrons in for the show. Hank the bartender nods and says, "In the dark, it won't look half bad."

He's lying, but his kindness is enough to release some of the tension in my chest. My barstool grates along the floor as I pull it out and sit.

"I see this a lot, you know," Hank says.

"What? Disaster?"

"Yes, but that's not exactly what I meant."

I pour another shot but don't drink it. "Yes, it is."

Shadows wind around the pillar of my glass, then melt into darkness. Hank allows me space and silence to consider my options until there is no time left to consider. The doorman, having assisted in prep and preened his slick green mohawk, yanks another stool by the door as the regulars filter inside and take their places at the bar. Hank leads me "backstage" to a supply room full of boxes and a mop, gives me a singular squeeze on the shoulder, and tells me to wait for his cue. I don't even know what that means, but I assume I'll know it when it comes.

My phone screen is black. No texts. No notifications. I pull up my chat with Jimothy and type *I miss you. Call me later* but delete it before sending. A sliver of me misses him. I want him to be proud of me, to think I am *someone* again. Someone interesting and fun and full of sex and cigarettes. I want to send him a pic of me in the dark and ask him where he thinks I am. Ask him what he thinks I am doing and make him say all the nasty things only I could get him to say.

He wouldn't say those things anymore, if I did text him. Not today. He'd only ask about Lola.

And if I'm being honest, I stopped asking him for such sweet reassurances long before Lola became the default.

I'm not sure how long I'm sitting there or exactly what is happening outside the room, but it takes Hank the bartender kneeling in front of me to shake me out of whatever trance cocoons me.

"Did you hear a fucking thing I said?" he asks.

My cue, I suppose.

Without another word I glide past him, out of the storeroom, and stumble onto the stage. The murmur of the bar dulls at the sight of me. What the fuck am I doing? What is wrong with me?

I *could* collapse, but I don't. Instead, I pretend I'm sitting on my rug at home, headphones pressing my ears into my skull until they go numb as a television drools sitcom banality in the background to disguise what I'm really doing from Lola. I tell myself I'm only practicing, crafting the thrill of the moment within the safe confines of my home. The controller is familiar here, easy and free. There is no smoke, no muted coughs from patrons in front of me, no clinking of glasses, no darkness. I am in my room with my headphones and my music, and damn if it isn't the loudest, most heart-skipping shit you've ever heard.

My opening song–a crisp French rager like a strobe light for the ears–blows the glasses off the nose of someone in the first row. Or that's what I see in my mind's eye. My light display, weak as it is, seems to pulse in rhythm with whatever I play, a sentient thing, appreciative of the care I've put into my choices. I feel one hundred feet tall, alone, in the sky on my own pedestal, breathing a kind of air I thought I'd aged out of. My buzz has long since faded, but Christ, I'm high as hell.

My set is short, just 30 minutes for a newbie like me. I fuck up with the crossfader on almost every single song and my glasses fly over the top my head as I crane my chin to the ceiling in some sensual fit of ecstasy. Sometimes a bizarre hiccup in my transitions sends the speakers into a spasm, but it doesn't matter. I fly through the set, fly through it, baby, and when I'm done I'm greeted with total fucking silence.

Who cares though? I nailed it, destroyed this stage. Every single pair of eyes drills into me. The staring feels like daggers in a vacuum absent of noise. Hank gapes at my feet, and when I look at myself I see a kaleidoscope of shattered plastic from one of the disco lights I apparently destroyed–don't know how or when, exactly, maybe during the clunky switch between my second and third song when I pounded the table, or maybe when someone booed at me and I considered, briefly, throwing the nearest strobe light at the audience in hopes I'd bloody the nose of whoever disrespected me. Another of the lights sits on its side, flashing predictable cop-like patterns onto the floor. It's hot to the touch, so I toss it over my shoulder and revel in the sound of the wooden floor demolishing its cheap, plastic shell.

I scream, woo-girl that room, spitting adrenaline onto the floor. Then, I glide off the stage, hopping down the foot-high barrier separating me from the audience. Before I can make back to the storeroom, someone from the back shouts that I fucking suck. This arouses a small wave of shadowy snickers.

"Who cares, nerd!" I say to the room before stomping out of view to collect myself.

The dark ought to calm me and slow the overflowing pot of hormones trembling through my veins, but it doesn't. Pearlescent blobs of color blur my vision so that I can't even make out the mop cart I know rests to my right. I'm seeing stars, an ocean of them, my body riding the crest of a huge wave. My hands ache as I unfurl my fists, pain the only indicator I'd been clenching them.

Someone–it's Hank–knocks on the closed door and says, "You're going to clean up that mess before you leave."

By the time I've mellowed enough to show my face, the bar is nearly empty. My set has chased them all out, but I don't care. A broom and dustpan rests against the stage alongside the rolling cart I'd used earlier to haul my gear. The shattered lights made a bigger mess than I thought. The glass of the bulbs seems to have disintegrated into a translucent snow, but I get everything I can see, load my gear on the cart, and wheel my way towards the exit.

"Hank," I say. He does not offer me a drink. "I'll be coming back."

He cocks his head to the side but offers no further affirmations, which I regard as a tacit acceptance of my proposal. The front door of the bar grates with a moan of relief as it shuts behind me, the dark of night selling the perception of chilliness even though I'm sweating through my shirt. It's late and I should be getting home. I have a kid, after all, and she's home alone, but I can't bring myself to return. My text to her goes unanswered, as does my message to Jimothy. I envision them chatting together without me. Conspiring.

Where's Mom?

Gone

Gone where?

Who knows?

My conjured image of Jimothy's glower follows me as I roll my stuff to the car. His disappointed grimace lingers over my shoulder as I hurl my equipment into the hatch and slide into the front seat. My grip keeps slipping from the wheel as I idle in the parking lot, my hands still buzzing with whatever high I'd slipped into on stage. I can't go home just yet–I might break something. Or worse yet, I might engage in conversation with my moody child.

So I drive under the pretense of needing gas even though my tank is half full; to me, half full might as well mean topped off because I don't bother refilling the tank until the light on the dash screeches a warning. I drive and drive, looking for a gas station in this odd part of town I'm not used to, then pulling into the first lit building with a pump I stumble upon. The parking lot is empty save one Toyota pickup.

While unleaded gas dribbles from its tank in the ground to the tank in my car, I find myself fiddling with my wallet. The drummer's license pokes out from behind my own. Calvin is an idiot man-boy with an idiotic face. The sight of him rises my tide of fury to its tipping point, distracting me from the scrawny white woman with a face like a wrinkled couch who is waddling towards me from the shadows.

The rasp in her voice is trenched into the flesh of her esophagus from years of abuse. She's got a limp in her right leg and stops just a few steps away. "You have change for the bus? I'll take anything."

"Buses don't run this late," I say.

"They run tomorrow, don't they?" The overhead lights cast a sickly glare off the sweat on her forehead. She reaches out a hand. "Please."

"I don't have any cash, sorry."

"Don't worry about it," she says, and her hands slip into the pocket of her hoodie, then emerge lazily with a switchblade in tow. "I take cards, too."

I've imagined moments like these many times in my life, wondering how I would react to being mugged or attacked, and I do know what I would do in *most* situations–run. I've always daydreamed about catastrophe, about exit plans *just in case*. Probably because I always knew that my survival relied solely on my own wits. My mother was too wasted to care about taking care of my safety; on the rare occasions she was sober in my presence, she was usually too hungover to be of any help when I needed her, anyway.

This sad woman with a knife is not who I envisioned as the perpetrator in my imaginary mugging scenario. Even her weapon is too big for her hands, tip pointing down because her wrists are too weak to keep proper aim.

I scan my surroundings. It's just her and me out here, except for the cashier inside, who must be completely disinterested in parking lot shakedowns. Hell, this old lady could be the cashier. It's difficult to tell with such bad lighting.

"Get the fuck out of here, lady. I'm not giving you anything."

The gas pump clunks off. It's quiet aside from the woman's wheeze. She blinks a few times, sizing me up.

"Give me your goddamn purse." There's no point arguing, so I make for the pump, setting the nozzle back in its cradle as if the woman did not exist. I think, stupidly, that this will be the end of it, that this woman will perceive my nonchalance as power and skulk away in search of another mark, but that's a power move only effective in suburbia. I should know better.

She lunges for me with surprising quickness, her bum knee nothing but a ruse. My back slams against the open gas cap of my Kia. The impact sends a sciatic jolt through my hip, and before I even understand what's come over me, I am screaming right back at her, loud enough that my voice starts to crack. The woman skitters back, knife bouncing on the concrete and out of reach. My temples burn with a delightful throb as my jaw pops.

I run at her, shoulder her sternum like a linebacker. The shove sends her backward, to the ground. Her head hits the concrete with a satisfying thwack. I waste no time straddling her, my knees pinning her arms to the asphalt. My lips are agape and drooling onto the front of her dirty shirt.

She glares death at me, then disgust as her eyes follow the slick of saliva dangling from my mouth to the wet spot on her chest. She looks so frail now, so pathetic, this strange woman, and I can't help but inch closer to get a better look at her as if she was a specimen in a lab. This close, I can see the wisps of youth on her; she isn't as old as I originally thought. Those marks on her body aren't wrinkles, they're scars. She's dehydrated, skin puckering like loose shrink wrap. Her body is ravaged, not aged. A woman like this probably won't live long enough to know what age feels like.

She spits in my face and curses.

I feel the *something* from the club drape over me like strings of drool, the same sensation I felt with the drummer. I'm in another dimension now and all I can see are the woman's cheap feather earrings, and I want them. I want those earrings. They look amazing.

So I get higher on top of her, maneuvering my knee from her elbow to her chest. Her expression slowly twists from white hot fury to something else. Fear, maybe (finally), and I like it.

"Give me your earrings," I say, my mouth sloppy and wet.

Her only response is a strained crease in her forehead as if hearing English for the first time, but I hold my hand out and repeat myself.

She says, "Take the knife. It's worth more."

"Earrings."

The woman's face purples like a bruise as she gasps for breath. "Take them," she tries to say, her voice failing before she can finish. How pathetic she is.

And her earrings are ugly things, matted together and dirty, but they slide quite easily out of her ears. No backs, just long loops that reach the bottom of the lobe. I wonder why she wears them at all–they must be uncomfortable, especially if she's sleeping on the streets. The feathers appear brown, but upon closer inspection I see peeks of canary yellow. The woman's chest stops heaving, even though I haven't released her from under my knee.

"Where did you get these?" I ask her.

"Fuck you." She can barely get the breath out, but her meaning is clear enough.

My muscles are twitching from exertion, so I lurch to my feet. The woman doesn't move.

Choosing my favorite of the pair, I toss the other earring into a puddle of gasoline by the pump. The feathers all but dissolve into the slick, and before the woman can resume her attack, I grab my wallet from the ground and lock myself back into my car.

Glancing back at her only once before fleeing the station, I see her kneeling under the pump cradling something–the remaining earring–in her palms, offering it to the sky, to God, in supplication. Stupid woman. Doesn't she know? God forgot about her a long time ago, but she'll just keep on praying like a fool, begging for scraps of attention that will never leave her sated.

The mate of her offering falls in between my front seats as the Kia jerks to the right. I'm on the road again, leaving the memory of the woman back in the oily shadows where I found her.

Chapter 8

Sleep steals away the next twelve consecutive hours, only freeing me from its vice grip at the nauseating scent of Lola cooking grilled cheese for lunch. My vision constricts to white as I rise too quickly out of bed; by the time sight returns, I am hovering over the kitchen table, my teenager glaring at me with an expression of pure bewilderment.

"Where were *you* last night?" she asks, though not as accusatorily as I expect. It strikes me that she might have been worried, which is an odd turn of events.

"I'm sorry. I should have called you." It's all I can think to say.

"Dad called."

"How's Grandma?"

"Not great, but you know that." Lola sits across from me, silently picking at her sandwich.

"Did you enjoy having the place to yourself last night?"

She shrugs, covering a reflexive smirk with a corner of bread.

"Good," I say. "That's good." I'm talking more to myself now, meandering toward the coffee machine before she senses my discomfort.

"Will you be home tonight?" she asks.

"Why?"

"Curious, is all."

"Got plans I should know about?"

She stuffs her mouth with food and shakes her head. Her expression is inscrutable.

I stick to espresso, even though it means I risk poking the beehive with the sound of the bean grinder. The espresso maker is an old machine that works about seventy percent of the time; today, it behaves. Water aggressively churns through its mechanism.

"Maybe we can watch a movie tonight?" I ask her, toeing the waters of my parental standing.

She finishes her sandwich before replying. "Only if I get to pick."

Espresso can't touch the malaise which haunts me today. I feel drenched and heavy, each flicker of my muscles a monumental stress on my weary body, as if invisible weights attach to my bones. Everything–every noise, even the sound of my own breathing–grates like a jet engine. I'm not even hungover. No headache, no stomach cramps. I'm just so thoroughly wiped it feels like I've invented a new type of exhaustion.

I drink four shots of espresso and immediately pass out on the couch, where I crash for the next six hours. The image of me splayed across the cushions, night shirt bunched up just under my tits and sleeping shorts askew where they stuck to my sweaty thighs, will be forever ingrained in my daughter's mind. Drool sticks my cheek to the couch leather, peeling away like a Ziploc bag as I drag myself up after my second hibernation of the day.

With nothing but coffee in my belly I am ravenous, but there is nothing in the house I want to eat. None of my staple snacks sound appealing. The thought of nibbling a plain piece of bread turns my stomach, which is unfortunate because that's about all we have in the house. I need to place another grocery order. I suppose I ought to feed my child, at least.

"Thai food tonight?" I yell upstairs, curious to see if Lola will respond. She does, but via text.

pad thai HOOOTTTTT

Nothing cures malaise better than the sinus blowout of extra spicy food. I order my usual yellow curry and wait by the front door for the delivery to arrive. When a boy of sixteen (at most) pulls up to the house, the sight of my disheveled ass stops him in his tracks. I realize then that I never bothered to put on proper clothes.

"Just leave it on the curb, kid," I growl. He obliges gratefully. His expression waffles between shock and amusement, and I can only assume he's texting his friends about the batshit lady whose extra spicy Thai food he just delivered.

Lola and I sit silently across the table from each other, her eating while I rearrange pieces of potato with my chopsticks. I manage to swallow one piece of carrot before giving up, but Lola wolfs her plate clean, down the last bean sprout. She then announces which movie she has chosen for tonight, and I know from the flirtatious flutter of her eyelashes it's something I am going to hate.

"You always use Dad as an excuse to never watch scary movies. Since he's not here, that's what I want to watch."

It's not that horror movies frighten me. They bore me to tears. But Lola is still clinging to her rare-form agreeability. Woe betide me to argue.

"What kind of scary movie?"

"Demons. Possessions. Pretty standard stuff."

"Is it part of a series?" Serialist horror irritates me. It leans more into shock and gore than story and the laziness dulls my interest. It's hard to be shocked and awed by the fourth film installment featuring yet another masked serial killer with a penchant for camp counselors–again. What are the odds?

She shrugs. "I don't think so, but I'm not going to spoil it by looking it up."

A defeated sigh slips out of my mouth, but I decide to jump wholly on board with our bonding adventure. "First one to hide behind a couch pillow does dishes."

She smirks, refusing to agree to a bet she knows she will lose.

With the leftovers securely tucked away in the fridge, I send Jimothy a quick text while Lola gets the movie set up.

She's onto me. Making me watch a horror movie because my excuse (you) is not here. I hope you're happy

Jimothy is quick to respond. Must be bored.

Good. I'm tired of taking all the heat

How's your mom

She forgot my name today. Not like those times when all the kids' names squirreled up in the head. I could tell she genuinely did not recognize me for a minute. It's weird. She's nicer

That is weird

"It's starting," Lola shouts from the other room.

Movie is starting. Talk to you tomorrow?

To this, my husband does not respond.

I settle into my usual spot on the couch and squint at the subtitles through the entire first half of the movie. It's filmed exclusively in the dark, with every scene allergic to a light switch, so I envision my own movie amongst the guttural wails of the possessed. The homeless woman's face from last night flashes behind my eyelids. I see her hands cradling her remaining earring. When the actress in the movie rakes her nails across the face of her lover, it's the gas station woman I see. I can't even remember specific features from the night before, but here and now, I am certain the woman on the screen is the same woman from last night. The actor playing her lover is the drummer Calvin, whose license burns like a cross in my wallet. I see the earring leaving a singed spot between the seats of my car, a graveyard where my stolen items lie.

Lola is too enraptured by the screen to notice my distress and for this I am grateful. She doesn't ask if she should pause the movie when I flee to "use the bathroom."

I look as exhausted as I feel. Dark bags tug at the bottom lids of my eyes so that I resemble a haggard bulldog. It's like I'm descending into an endless tunnel, burrowing myself into the dirt, hiding under the bones of my old life. A demon. A thing lying in wait now emerged, furious and hungry. Remembering my escapades of the night before, specifically my performance, conjures a surge of vomit to the back of my throat. I swallow it down to keep from worrying Lola. I need an exorcist before this midlife crisis eats me alive.

My child shouts from the other room, something about me *missing it*, and I bury a scream into a hand towel before returning to the couch. The movie is a monotonous drone. It grates like cymbal crashes, when all I really want at this moment is silence. Quiet. Rest. The audacity of this movie to interrupt my rest makes my chest tighten.

The "it" I missed was the possessed woman ripping through her restraints and hurtling towards her lover as a priest chants incantations at the pulpit. With both clawed hands, the woman rips her lover's throat clean out of his body. As he gurgles to his death, the woman turns to the priest and snaps him in half. The screen fades to black as the man screams for his life, brightening into a timelapse as the woman shops for groceries. An orange rots in her hands, and she tosses it into her cart and smiles.

I can guess the director, studio, and everyone else who helped make this trash is hoping to appeal to young women just like Lola. The heroine is rotten, yes; she has killed people, yes; she continues to poison everything she touches. This is all supposed to be a good thing. Or, an empowering thing, at least, which should be something I'd enjoy, or at least agree with.

Maybe I just don't like the message because somebody else said it.

My daughter watches enraptured as the credits roll, only speaking once the screen reverts to the streaming home page.

"What did you think?" she asks.

And I don't know what to say. I *think* it was a pandering, tactless mess with a very bloated special effects budget. The movie did manage to upset me, though. In its clueless way, it did touch on something. The image of the shriveling orange lingers on my tongue like cod liver oil: repulsive, but potent beyond all imagining.

"It definitely gives me something to think about, even if by accident," I say.

"So you hated it." She tries to hide her disappointment, but the droop of her lower lip is unmistakable.

"I didn't hate it, honestly, I didn't. I mean, you know how I am with scary movies, Lola."

"I know," she says. "You *did* watch it with me even though you didn't like it. Is that what parenting is like?"

"Parenting is being obsessed with your child. A person can do a lot of crazy, mind-numbing, senseless shit in pursuit of an obsession."

"That's weird, Mom."

"Talk to me when you have kids. Then you'll get it."

She shifts in her seat, tucking a leg underneath her. "Emily's mom said her love for her kids is like nature begging her to survive. Like, for her genes to be carried on. She used the word *primal.*"

"Primal? Yeah, I guess that's a good word for it. But the rest is nonsense."

"I don't know. Maybe you both could be right."

"Why this line of questioning suddenly? You aren't pregnant, are you?" I regret the question even before it lands. Lola's face contorts into a visage of disgust.

"No, Mom! How could you think that?"

"I'm not accusing you of anything. Your questions are just odd."

"You're the odd one, Mom," Lola says as she jumps up from the couch. "*You're* odd. I was just trying to talk to you."

"That's what I thought we were doing!" I recover myself too slowly, too late to repair the damage. And if I wasn't completely clear on Lola's stance already, the swift slam of her door certainly cements it.

Once again, I am an icon of stellar parenting.

Chapter 9

Monday springs upon me like a beast, announcing the morning with the offensive clang of my alarm. My weekend activities seem like they happened in another lifetime, but then again, walking into my office always has a way of wiping all the color out of a room. To add to my misery, I am sickened to find out that Cassandra will be coming to my location for an in-person meeting this afternoon. This prompts me to do something I usually avoid at all costs: speak to one of my coworkers.

The girl one cubicle over is my first choice. She's young, putting herself through community college, and generally quiet. I'm banking on our age difference and my general lack of congeniality to keep the conversation brief and to the point, but I am wrong.

I've not even fully risen from my seat when she's making eyes at me, rumor wetting her hungry lips. "Did you hear?" she says. "Cassandra is coming."

"I heard. Do you know why?"

"She said for a meeting, but you know her. That could mean anything." The ding of her messenger app darts her attention to her screen. Her sticky mouth twists into a knowing expression. The way her lips purse makes me feel feral. She knows something that I don't.

"What?" I ask.

"It's nothing. Samantha asked me what I want for lunch today."

This is a lie, but I can't call her out because then I'd have to admit that I have no clue which person is Samantha. I've stopped bothering with their faces. The older I get, the younger my coworkers seem. After a while all these young girls look like the same, round-faced little girl wearing her mommy's heels.

I'm about to return to my desk when the girl offers one flimsy teaser. "You know, Cassandra talks about you all the time."

Ah, so this is why she's in town. A meeting with me, or perhaps my direct boss to discuss my behavior? Or maybe just to plan another party for herself to which I will be her designated planner. Who knows? "All good things, I'm sure."

She smirks. "I'm sure."

I want to slap her across her arrogant little cheeks, but my mood cools when I acknowledge the exchange is my own fault. I shouldn't have said anything. This is why I avoid work conversations at all costs. Everyone here is annoying, and I am too much of a grouchy bitch to let anything slide. It doesn't help that I am the oldest one at this level by more than a decade. Everyone else my age is management, a fact I wear like a badge of honor.

The prospect of sitting face-to-face with Cassandra in any capacity makes my skin crawl. If she somehow weaseled her way into a seat at a disciplinary meeting for me, I might snap the conference table in half. Now, I know I shouldn't stew or make hasty assumptions. There could be a multitude of reasons for her arrival, but I can't help it. By lunch, I am so suffused with fury that my vision is blurring. If they intend to fire me, they should just send me an email and have me escorted out. I don't need a condescending lecture on top of it.

My manager, McKenzie, floats through the room, leaning into the cubicle of another employee. Is that Samantha? Who knows. I swear McKenzie's gaze lingers a beat longer on me than the rest of the room. My pen is slippery in my fingers–I'm sweating like a tea kettle. I'm about to burst.

Then, instead of exploding, an eerie calm falls over me like cold water. I achieve clarity all at once and I feel stupid, so stupid, for not reaching this conclusion years ago.

My cubicle is practically bare, absent of adornment. There's one picture of me cradling baby Lola and a Polaroid of Jimothy and I back when we first met, clinking together shot glasses of Jägermeister. Subconsciously, I must have known I would someday leave this place in a huff.

The Polaroid is the only thing I bother taking with me. I have a million pictures of Lola. They can keep this one. I'm halfway to the door before anyone notices.

"Going on lunch?" someone asks–I don't know who, and I don't care.

"Yup," I say. "And I quit."

I consider adding a little 'eat shit' farewell for Cassandra, but the insult isn't worth my time. Nothing in this place is worth my time. In fact, I don't even know what we do here anymore. Might as well leave and let them find some new blood, an employee who will at least pretend to care for a while. I've got more important things to tend to.

As I leave the parking lot in front of my office building one final time, I select Hank's number and hit the call button. He does not answer, so I am forced to leave a voicemail.

"Hank, I've suddenly found myself in possession of a lot more time. Call me. This is Disco Mama."

Chapter 10

Why stop with a voice message? Before Hank can decide whether or not to call me back, I drive down to the Rat House and am first through the door when the bar opens.

Getting him to allow me back on stage takes some cajoling, but he eventually agrees with specific terms:

- No breaking equipment on stage.
- Only one call to his cell allowed, and only within one week of my set.
- Fifty dollar fine for every time I jump-scare him.
- No calling the audience "nerds."

I solemnly swear to uphold all our agreed-upon tenets of performing and leave the Rat House feeling ten pounds lighter than when I entered. The drive home is a blur of set lists and big dreams.

My joy makes Lola suspicious. She watches me word-lessly as I flit through the pantry looking for something to make for dinner. She is so wary of my happiness that she neglects to inform me of her very important lunch-time conversation from her father until after we finish our quesadillas.

"He's coming home," Lola says.

I'm reading the label on a bag of tortillas without fully comprehending what she is saying. "Huh?"

"Have you talked to Dad yet?"

"What? Yeah, of course. Wait–today? No. I don't think I have." In fact, I haven't checked my notifications even once since leaving work this afternoon. As if on cue, my phone buzzes from within my purse.

"What did he say?"

"Grandma is doing better. He found a good hospice for her. Has a buyer on the house, I guess. He says he's coming home soon."

"How soon?" I ask.

Lola stares at me as if I've spoken in another language before answering. "He didn't say."

"This is good news," I say, even though it is not good news. This is bad news. Bad timing, at the very least. Jimothy will lose his mind when he finds out I've quit my job on a whim. He most definitely will not understand my new obsession and he will certainly come unglued to learn I've been leaving our teenager at home alone to pursue it. Jimothy coming home means death to all the little sprouts of hope I've planted. This simply will not do.

Lola excuses herself, disappearing to her room with her nose in her phone. I know she is texting and I resist the urge to ask her who she's talking to. I imagine it is Jimothy and she's telling him how strange I've been acting over the past three or so weeks, begging him to come home. Or maybe it's Emily's mom, consoling my child in a way I can never manage. Or maybe it's Calvin, regaling her again with his absurd story about how her mother ate his driver's license right in front of him. Maybe she's starting to believe him.

I can't focus on hypotheticals right now–I must speak with my husband.

He answers after one ring.

"I've been trying to call you all day!"

"I know, I know. Sorry. It was just one of those days. Lola tells me you're coming home soon, yeah?"

He's quiet a beat longer than normal and says, "How are things going at home?"

"What's that supposed to mean?"

He sighs in a way I haven't heard him sigh in years. Not since our breakup way back when, after I decided he was getting too close and I wasn't in the mood to be caged by his feelings. He says, "Lola keeps asking when I'll be back, but when I ask her if everything is okay, she won't say anything. Do you know of any reason she might be upset?"

"Have you ever considered that she just misses her father?"

"I mean, yes. But this seems different."

His ambiguity sucks all the sweetness from my voice. "Different how? Or is it just that you don't trust me with my own kid?"

"That's not what I said."

What a liar. "Then what?"

"Have *you* ever considered that I miss my family?"

"Then why lead like an interrogator? Just say you miss us and you're coming home. Must you pick at my self-confidence in the process?"

The line is so silent that, for a second, I am certain he's hung up on me. I'd have respected him more if he had.

"I'm sorry," he says. "You're right and I'm sorry. Maybe I'm just reading too much into things because I'm so far away, and I'm with my mother. Turns out she's just as intolerable when she doesn't know who I am as when she does."

Ah, now I understand. He isn't really sorry: he needs something from me.

"It's not going very well, is it?" I ask knowing that it is not. He is looking to find a crisis at home so he has a reason to get away from Marilyn.

He and his mother used to be close. As the other brothers put it, Jimothy was the favorite by a country mile. But then he reconnected with me and met my feral daughter, and we stole him away. Marilyn has spent every waking second since driving a wedge between herself and her son. The wound is so deep that not even her deathbed could bring them back together. I wonder what kind of things she's saying to face without realizing who he is.

"If we make it out of escrow without the deal completely collapsing, I am out of here. I got her into a good place: Oaktree Retirement Community. They have an apartment complex on site for the residents who need round-the-clock care. I thought I might stay in town longer just to make sure she is settled, but I don't know if I have it in me. A hotel isn't far enough away. All I think about is seeing her again the next morning."

He has gone far beyond the requirements of a son to an abusive mother. His brothers contribute nothing but excuses. This is the time when Jimothy must relieve himself of the burden of caretaker's duties so that he is prepared for when Marilyn dies and every scummy relative in his life emerges from under their rocks for their share. I should say this to him. I should encourage him to return. This is the reason for his call: he needs me to say it to make his choice acceptable. But I don't. I can't. I have far too much to do, and I can't come clean. Jimothy being who he is, will either insist I go to therapy or, even worse, try to help. Music has always been one of the binding agents between us, which means he would mistake my setlists for a musical theory debate that I just don't have the patience for. I need more time–alone.

All the same, I hate myself for what I'm about to say. If it wasn't for my ulterior motives, I'd never dream of squashing Jimothy, but I'm a selfish woman. That guilt is for Tomorrow-Me, that is if I feel any at all.

"Will you regret it if you leave?"

This might be a legitimate question if either of us had healthy emotional attachment styles, but we don't. I can hear the cudgel land as the effective blow it was intended to.

"I don't know," he says. I know that, in yet another small way, I've broken his heart again. He will not be coming home any time soon.

I backpedal. "I just want you to make sure you're making the best decision for you right now. She's a monster, but you aren't, and God forbid something happen right after you leave. I just–I don't want you to have any doubts about yourself. I also know that you will never allow anyone to comfort you if you *do* start blaming yourself, which you *shouldn't*, but you will."

Even from another state, I can clearly see the way his face curdles. This is not what he hoped for, but his emotional needs do not deter me from pursuing what I want. It never has.

We end the call, and I pray to whoever might be listening that Marilyn stays alive at least another few weeks. It's the least she could do for me.

Chapter 11

The sour memory of my first performance turns my thoughts to the next one. If I'm going to find any success in this gig, I probably need real help from people who know what they are doing. I considered briefly chumming the waters at various clubs for someone with experience, but the thought of begging twenty-something burnouts for help doesn't sit right with me. (I remember being a twenty-something burnout, which is how I know I've graduated into the face of "the Man" by default, just by aging. They'll rip my throat out with rabid teeth.) Bedroom practice isn't cutting it, and since there is no store called Deejaying for Forty-Somethings, I find myself outside of Best Buy. Maybe there is a molly-rolling teenager with big dreams working in the computer department. I need someone who doesn't mind wearing a uniform.

This was my fourth department store attempt of the day.

The building is empty, save for a handful of employees and one older man rifling through the discount DVD bin.

I take my time wandering through each section before spotting my target. He looks about Calvin's age and has a full sleeve of Metallica tattoos. I don't know what it is about Metallica, but their fans are passionate things who have poor taste in favorites, but tend to love many genres of music. I've never met a Metallica fan that I couldn't engage in a musical theory debate that ends with each of us becoming the other's mortal enemy. They're fun.

My selected employee senses my approach the way a street cat senses a loose toddler looking for something to squeeze. He stares at his phone as if getting a very important message. If I was anyone else, I might move along to a more amenable employee, but unfortunately for Metallica Boy, it's him I am looking for.

"Excuse me," I say, stepping close enough in front of him to blow aside the hair draping over his eyes.

I think about what I am about to ask and realize how ridiculous it sounds. *Excuse me, I know I'm wearing stained khakis, but I am also a DJ who knows nothing about deejaying. You're a hip, young fellow. Help a granny out?*

So, I pivot. "My nephew wants to be a DJ."

This statement seems to have caught him off guard. "A DJ?"

"Yeah. He's into it very suddenly and I want to support him. His dad died a few months ago and I'm hoping he can channel his grief into something. You know how sixteen-year-olds can be."

The lie spills out easily, surprising even me, so much so that this imaginary nephew's face begins to shape into a real boy–sandy-haired and sullen, just like his imaginary dead dad. Handsome fella, too.

But before I can get too invested in my fake family, the Best Buy employee waves me away. "I'm sorry, but I really don't know anything about deejaying. I just sell TVs."

"Is there anyone here who would know?"

He folds his arms in front of him, as if to ward off further inquisition. "No."

What a waste of a good Metallica tattoo.

"Fine, then," I say in my most mom-infused voice, and I hope he understands just how thoroughly he has disappointed me. I hope my rancid face clings to him like bad morning breath.

The sliding doors of the exit whoosh open as I cross the threshold into the parking lot, when a voice behind me catches my attention.

"Ma'am. Hey, lady! Ma'am. Miss!"

I turn to see the most curious little creature plummeting toward me: a petite human, closer in age to my child than to me, whose skin is blanched by the bright blue of her uniform, stops just short of me, huffing and out of breath.

"I heard you're looking for a DJ."

"I'm looking for the equipment," I say while simultaneously checking to see if I'm bugged. There is no way this girl could have heard my conversation with Metallica Boy.

"What do you need?" she gasps. The square nametag on her polyester shirt says CRIS and is decorated with two tattered rainbow stickers.

"How did you hear about my request?"

Cris looks away, then at the air above me, then at my shoes. "Alex is an asshole."

Alex must be Metallica Boy. "Did he say something over the radio?"

"Yeah, but he sucks and no one likes him, so I wouldn't take it personally."

"And what makes you chase me into the parking lot, Cris?" I don't tell her how fascinating she is to me. Her small, soft voice immediately magnetizes my attention like a wayward chick's peep catches a hen's ear. My answer already feels like a yes–but I want to know what she is up to first.

"I'm a DJ," she says. "And I really think I can help your nephew."

"You understand that there is no nephew, right?"

She blows her brown bangs away from her eyes in the manner of someone who's been fed up with other people their entire life.

"I really don't give a shit, ma'am," she says, pulling a phone from her back pocket. "My cousin does weddings and bar mitzvahs and stuff like that. I work with him on weekends sometimes. What's your number?"

"I'm not really interested in weddings," I say.

"Neither am I, but he just says 'that's the job.'"

"You don't like playing at weddings and you know I'm full of shit. So why did you chase me down?"

A sly grin sneaks across her face and I see a glimmer of my younger self. This girl is bad. As if to confirm my intuition, she says, "I don't know. You made Alex really uncomfortable, and I hate Alex so I figured we might get along."

She starts to put her phone away, but I stop her hand and recite my number before she changes her mind.

"Cris," I ask. "Have you ever been to the Rat House?"

❖ ❖ ❖

Cris's cousin, who is old enough to be her uncle but soft enough to let Cris pull off a stunt with a weird lady she met at her part-time job, owns Party Town DJs! (the exclamation point is included in their trademark. He made sure to emphasize that.) Cris's explanation was completely accurate and true: he mainly handles weddings and birthday bashes and the like.

"Never one for the club scene," he says. "No money in it unless you're famous, but Cris refuses to give it up."

I didn't know what to do when he shot me a commiserating look like *kids, am I right?* as if I wasn't the one dousing gasoline onto his little cousin's wildfire dreams. I decided to say nothing because he let us make use of five thousand dollars' worth of equipment for only two hundred. Cris didn't charge me a thing up front; I suspect she'll bill me if I'm satisfied with tonight's performance and want to book her services again. She's knowledgeable in every way, from vinyl to our crummy venue. Turns out my little protégé (mentor?) *has* been to the Rat House, or at least that's what she says. She seems even less impressed by it in person than she was when we agreed to work together in the Best Buy parking lot.

"It helps to be old enough to drink," I say.

She makes a face that indicates she doesn't believe a word I say before glossing over to the topic at hand: tonight's show. I can't help but think she and Lola would become fast friends, but I wouldn't dream of introducing them. They would probably gang up and eat me, piece by piece.

Cris and I have run through the set a dozen times, always meeting at Party Town DJs! on her days off from Best Buy. She runs me through the software she uses, which is much more user friendly than the DIY DJ app I was using before. I especially take to fading. The effect of seamlessly melting songs together, stretching the vibe, thrills me. I tend to redline often, which is when all the audio lights turn red and sound gets distorted. Doing it too much can blow out the speakers. I spend most of my time with the controller training myself not to do that.

Before I know it, the performance day is here. Hank was very unhappy to hear I've employed a crew–that is, until Cris reversed her cousin's trailer to the back door and started hauling some real-deal shit towards the stage.

My hands are trembling, and I ask Hank for a drink to give my fingers something to hold onto. It seems like an eternity has passed, though it's only been one month. Maybe it's because when I was on my own, I could chalk my failure up to my impulsivity. To being reckless. Nerves, probably. Now that things are getting serious, I'm more anxious for my sophomore show than my first.

The gear Cris shimmies into place (strong thing, she is, refusing my help out of pride and too naïve to realize how rarely I offer it) only exacerbates my sense of inexperience. I pray I do all the gear justice, because to fuck up now would only prove that I have no business being here at all, and quitting my job was in vain, and manipulating Jimothy into spending more time in Utah was not only cruel, but pointless. To be honest, I myself am vague about how this new passion rooted itself inside me so thoroughly and so quickly. I just know that I want to do this, and I am tired of not being able to do what I want.

I feel like I'm standing in chest-deep water already and the levee is about to burst, one way or another. It's moments like these where I wish I was still a smoker. In theory, a cigarette sounds like a balm, something to soothe. This is because smokers are anxious every moment they don't have a cigarette between their fingers–nicotine is both the problem and the solution.

So instead of smoking, I head to my car under the pretense of forgetting my phone. I grab a pillowcase from the passenger seat and open it. I've kept its contents hidden even from Cris, who knows every other intimate detail of Disco Mama's existence. It feels juvenile to hide it, but something inside me wants to keep it all to myself for as long as possible. I want to surprise everyone–even the ones who think they know it all.

One week ago, after a long night of practice with Cris, she and I got to talking about music. She loves Oingo Boingo as much as I do, which only endears her to me further. She said I should try and work "Dead Man's Party" into a set if this all takes off, which got me thinking about how I should measure my success. I don't want to take over the world. I just want to feel part of it again. Really, I just want people to listen to me, any amount of people, but the more, the better.

My first set was competent, but discordant. I plucked songs out of my favorites playlist and slapped them in whichever order felt right, and it showed. It lacked a theme, which is a mistake I won't repeat. The Rat House is hardly larger than a convenience store with standing room enough to fit in a bathroom stall. This audience can't move, they can't dance and pump fists and mosh or whatever coked-out crowds like to do these days. The show needs to be mellow but hypnotic, must be something they can sway and sing along to. It needs to be something they feel comfortable getting drinks in the middle of, all while keeping one eye on me, for fear of missing something. Ambiance only. I want to infect the crowd, make them forget their own name.

Besides, a glut of dollar-store DJs already exists, all of them with more know-how than me. I don't want to compete with them. Even if that was the plan, I'd never win. I need to separate myself from them right off the bat. On top of good music, I also need a *persona*.

The day following that conversation with Cris, I went to the craft store and bought one hundred dollars' worth of Styrofoam, sequins, glue, and black mesh. Then I stopped at Party City for a cheap mask that would cover my entire face (a deer mask, of all things, just because I liked the slimming slope of the chin area). The item in the back of my car is the result of many nights of secret craft work on the floor of my bathroom. I stole the design from one of my favorite albums, which features a scantily clad human with a snake's head. The band is called The Feather Dusters. Disappointing how I only like one song from their entire first album, but, what a song it is. I avoided using it in this set out of some bizarre embarrassment, as if someone in the audience would put it all together and declare me a fraud. To be honest, I'd be shocked to find another fan of theirs in a crowd of thousands. They aren't that great besides their one, perfect gem. And their album cover.

I jabbed the dark eyes of the doe out with a box cutter, glued mesh over the holes, removed the antlers, then bejeweled the hell out of it. The finished piece is a shiny, silver mask with deep maroon vertical slits covering the eyes. I fell in love with it as soon as it was finished. *This* is

Disco Mama's reptilian face. It will look incredible from the stage, as long as the lights stay dimmed.

Cris wedges herself through the door of the bar and shouts for me to get moving, so I gather up my mask and head inside, thanking the fates, the universe, even God Himself for bringing Cris into my life. With her at the technological helm, I can focus on everything else. Even my name, Disco Mama, is beginning to grow on me. I just needed to steep in the name a bit to taste its potent flavor. Now, it no longer leaves an elderly aftertaste on my tongue and becomes more pretentious with every utterance. Disco Mama is an authority. She is *Mother.* She tells you what to do and you sit your ass down and learn.

"Light check," Cris says, indicating for me to get into place.

We run through the beginning of the set five times before Cris is satisfied. Everything must be synced to the second, and despite her youth, I trust her instincts completely. She doesn't fuck around when it comes to her passions, and neither do I.

Before I know it, we are thirty minutes out from show time. My hands no longer tremble but my mind still thinks they do. Adrenaline kicks my entire body into a state of hyper-vigilance. I smell and hear everything–every bad cologne and raspy smoker's cough. Glass clinks behind the bar as Hank serves his early guests. Unlike my first show, the place is packed tonight. Standing room only. A sea of scalps crowds the stage, so thick I could make my entrance by walking atop their heads. Instead, I wait in the broom closet.

I'm buzzing all over, my mind delirious in its attempt to soothe my body. The sensation is an old one, originating from the ancient part of my animal brain. My brain floods my body with some kind of hormone that makes my skin sting with alertness. The very act of breathing feels like thunder in my chest. There could be a pack of lions outside the door or a packed audience–my nerves can't distinguish between the two because they both trigger my fight-or-flight response. Good thing I loathe running or else I might never make it to the stage. My mask covers my face like the strong hand of an attacker muffling a scream. It resets the panic and forces me to take stock of my surroundings.

And then it's time. Cris knocks on the door of the storeroom three times, and gasps when I open to greet her.

"Did you make that?" she asks.

"Start the fog," I say, and once she turns away I snap my goggles into place. Time to light this place on fire.

I know that I'm on to something the moment I slip through the smoke and into view. Barstools creak, the people in them craning their heads to see. The music thrums low for the moment, a dirty sounding melody tailor-made for a place like this. I have twenty seconds to get them hooked before the light show begins. My fingers are still. There is little for me to do right now but watch the audience, and I am delighted to see all eyes on me, because how could they not look? Even if they hate me, I am too weird to ignore. The first beat drops and whoosh, we are off. I snare them with a rainbow of lights dribbling down the spectrum in perfect harmony with the music, and my chest unwinds just like last time until I forget where I am, because it's all music. Just music.

The electronic sound sweeps me away into the world inside my head, deep into the imaginary place I found inside myself when I was a kid, when I would dream about being a sorceress who controlled every insect on the planet and commanded them to swarm and eat her enemies. I am not a mother or a wife. I am not unemployed. I am the purveyor of mood, bass drilling my will into the chests and minds of the audience. There is so much power in my music and I slurp it up until my body buzzes with it and I just want to break shit again. Instead, I sway with the beat. The lights shining on my mask must look spectacular.

Every shift of the lights hits my veins like a needle. What a fucking high. I love this shit. My God, do I love this so much. In my peripherals, Cris signals our fifteen-second cue for a track change. She hovers just out of sight, manning an impressive control board for sound and lights. She is all business, determined, but even she rolls her shoulders with the tempo on occasion. The audience–my captives–do not budge. Not one of them. I take great care to snap my attention towards anyone who might try. *Buy a drink now? No, bitch, you are mine, sit the fuck down.* It's comical how simple it is to intimidate full grown adults with nothing but forceful eye contact. Thirty minutes passes like the fog of an anesthetic.

My set may have begun in the gutters, but it finishes in the stars. The final song picks up after a thoughtful lull in activity. Before my last selection begins, dim white lights nearing exsanguination roll into the room like wedding confetti. If you're paying attention, you can catch the glitter on your tongue. I call it my 'gold song' because of its shimmery seventies feel. It reminds of roller rink music, something teenage girls and boys would hold hands, a prelude to pubescent fondling and puppy love. The gold song makes me feel like howling–it's a malicious heart palpitation no one notices until it makes them cough.

Cris drops the lights as the final wisps of the gold song drool away, and by the time the house lights return I've fled the stage. Gone like a ghost, because I want to haunt them. I don't wait around for a reaction, although I hear someone say, "I thought you said she sucked?"

My hearing dulls as blood surges through my body. My vision blurs white on the edges, and I catch my clothes on the door handle of the storage room just before falling on my ass. Sweat glues my shirt to my skin. I want to tear it off. It feels like the hot flashes I used to get during my pregnancy. That kind of heat is unbearable, like baking a small sun in your uterus. Then again, I am in my forties. This could be menopause. Could be a million things. Could be—

Cris rips the door open and pours into the closet, hands snatching my shoulders, delight drawn all over her face. "That was amazing," she says. "You were awesome."

But one glare from me sucks all her joviality from her face.

"Are you sick?" she asks.

I summon every ounce of motherly calm in my arsenal to appear calm and collected for this audacious youth. "No, I'm fine. I promise. Just coming down."

Go play with your toys while Mommy rests.

Thankfully, she leaves me alone, presumably to protect her equipment from drunks.

I am interrupted again almost immediately. This time, it's Hank, announcing himself with a polite but authoritative knock.

"You can't stay in there all night," he says through the door.

I quell the immediate urge to snap at him by biting my finger. Hard. I hear my skin tear before I feel it, like I'm ripping into a well-done steak with a dull knife. I need to break something, create hurt, even if to myself. An incontrollable viciousness takes hold of me, as if the heavy bass vibrated the key in my chest and unlocked the rage I've been stuffing down since I was a kid.

Blood trickles from the tip of my finger. I've broken the skin. Then, I open the door.

Hank spots the blood immediately. "You cut yourself. I have a first aid kit behind the bar. Now get out of here."

I mistakenly assume the Rat House will have cleared out after my set, like the last time I performed. I am wrong. People bubble around the counter, lines sprouting from both ends as Hank and the doorman try to keep up with the sudden swell of orders. No one sees me in the shadows of the hallway. If Cris is still here, she must be crushed by the mob. Blood from my bitten finger drips down my pant leg and onto my sneakers, and I'm cursing myself for not controlling my irritation-driven urges when the back door swings open and Cris saunters in dragging a dolly behind her.

"Hey," I say, suddenly aware of my exposure to the crowd. Lola comes here. Her friends come here. Are any of them here right now? The thought of some punk-ass teenager blowing my cover replaces all the blood in my body with murderous thoughts.

"Hey, Cris," I repeat.

She turns toward the noise, palming her hip as she spots me. She sasses me, "Should I also load everything by myself, or do you plan to help?"

My hand does all the talking before I can respond. The wound is positively gushing now. Cris's stricken expression makes me look again at what I've done to myself, and my plateauing adrenaline clarifies the severity of it. I've bitten my finger nearly to the bone. My teeth shredded the skin like I was a rabid mongrel. The wound already looks diseased, and I've only just done it. A pool of blood blooms around my right sneaker directly under my hanging hand.

"Holy shit. That's bad."

Cris unties her sweatshirt from her waist and throws it at me. "Use this."

"There's a lot of blood," I say. "I'll ruin your hoodie."

"Buy me another one," she says before disappearing to collect the rest of her gear.

I wander through the back door and into the alley toward my car, Cris's sky-blue sweatshirt turning purple with my blood. Inspecting it closer, I realize it's her high school basketball team jacket. Is she still in high school? Where the hell are her parents? Not that I'm a model mother, but at least I know my child is home.

Probably.

My phone vibrates as if on cue and I seize it in a panic. The mere thought of talking to my husband has me feeling like a child again.

No sir, I'm doing my homework like a good girl. Oh yes, Husband. I'm at home right now, knitting mittens. Jimothy would never have married a woman who liked to knit, and I don't know why I'm thinking about him in this way now. Or why I pretend he ever wanted me tamed.

Jimothy and have two first dates. Two first encounters. Two different origins, depending on who is listening. The second meeting, the one that launched our marriage, began at a Walmart. I'd spent my last few dollars buying boxed macaroni and cheese with a whiny toddler on my hip, when I heard someone calling my name. It was Jimothy. The man that got away all those years ago. He asked about Lola, who spontaneously called him "Daddy," out of nowhere. She'd never done that to any man before. He laughed and responded that he was just a friend. And I seized the moment. I told him he *was* her daddy, even though I knew it was a lie. He, too, must have known it was a lie. It didn't matter in the end; he's certainly her dad now.

The real story begins and ends under the purple light of the Factory, a tumor of a nightclub disguised as a used record store by day. Really, it was a used record store that derelicts like me insisted upon being an exclusive night-time trap house for all our drug addict buddies to congregate in without being arrested. A friend of a friend was cousins with the owner; the kind of man who eventually mutates into that uncle your parents warn you to avoid. He smoked crack back then, as did many of the others. Personally, I never understood the allure of crack–it's hell on the skin–but that never hindered my attraction to their kind.

The building was far enough away from decent society to remain relatively unmolested by the cops. Occasionally, if our ranks swelled to levels of menacing infection, they might pop in for a quick bust meant to hit a quota. As far as they were concerned, we were small-time, not worth the ink in their ballpoint pens, as long as we stayed within the confines of our self-erected corral. Drugged cattle trotting unassisted through the front doors of the slaughterhouse, as it were.

The crew of the Factory was irregular, unreliable, and fleeting. People appeared and disappeared as quickly as a smoke break, so it wasn't unusual to find new faces every weekend. Some of them remained behind as "temporary regulars," while others floated in on the heels of the familiar, each as unmemorable as a shadow. Jimothy was one of those people, at first. If he'd attended the Factory a dozen times or just that one night, I couldn't say. He was about as noticeable as cardboard until he wasn't.

He'd asked for a smoke in the way vanilla people ask to bum a cigarette without exposing their suburban underbellies. The harder they try, the easier they are to spot, but I didn't mind. I'd been smoking menthols outside for an hour, mind drifting, trying to convince myself that I was freezing my ass off. The company was nice. He was warm. I leaned into him, cognizant of the implications, but I was so cold I didn't care. Forty-nine degrees Fahrenheit delivers like the Arctic when you live in the desert.

"You spend a lot of time outside," he said.

"I spend a lot of time smoking." I expected him to choke on his first drag, but he didn't. He sucked it down like the best of us.

"I'm Jimmy."

"Sure thing," I said. The truth was that I didn't care to know him beyond this moment. Introducing myself seemed like a waste of breath.

I can't recall what else we talked about out there. Music, probably. He dragged a fleet of airliners from mysterious pockets on the inside of his coat, and we drank them, mostly fireball whiskey because it was as cheap then as it is now. I threw up once then and again after my first attempt to rally; he led me to his car and drove me home. Later, I asked how he knew my address and he said I shouted directions at him for an hour until it dawned on him that "Winchoff Eyes" meant Glacial Pines, as in the Glacial Pines Apartments, which was located a five-minute walk from the Factory.

It was months before we crossed paths again, this time at a goth club downtown. I was there with my dealer and a couple other scrubs he dragged out of the gutters for the occasion. Jimmy was there with a girl. Pink hair. Eyeliner as thick as my pinky orbited her paper-white eyes. She was the type of girl who dons a junkie's uniform and thinks it makes her hard. I wondered how long they'd been dating, if this was their first night together or if I had been an illicit flirt a few months back. I was talking myself out of approaching them–because who was this guy? Why the fuck did I care?–when Jimmy noticed me noticing him and removed all my agency.

We fucked that night, and every night afterward for two months. No matter what we told people later–both before and after our wedding–we both knew the truth about how our relationship started. I always told Jimothy I preferred the first story, the original. The real one. The truth, inspected under the clarifying lens of maturity, is that I hated them both. I was crazy, he was crazy about me, and is it any surprise that our life together took such a fucked-up turn?

Back in the present, I check my phone and am relieved to see that the notification is not a text not from Jimothy, but a reminder I'd set weeks ago.

Company meeting tomorrow. Don't be late again, dipshit.

I laugh as I let myself into the Kia's driver seat. No more meetings for me. (Fuck you, Cassandra). I am delirious. Delighted, in fact. How wonderful to never have a mandatory meeting ever again. What a treat! The consequences don't matter. How will I explain my empty bank account to my husband? Who cares? He won't even notice for at least another week. Besides, he's not even here. He's in Utah with his mom, being the dutiful son to a terrible woman, and it suddenly clicks why I'm so elated, so buzzed by all this. It's because he's gone. His absence is like a cinder block off my chest; one I placed there myself, sure, but still. It's gone.

Gone.

The phone slithers from my bloody, bitten fingers, wedging itself between the seats. Something sharp pricks my skin as my hands dive to retrieve it. The earring. The one I stole from that homeless crone who tried to rob me. The matted feather is clotted with my blood. My hand is oozing, turning the entire piece a bright, healthy red. I wonder briefly what that woman is up to now. Is she robbing someone else, getting stoned in an alley, laid up in a hospital bed, or even dead? I think about her holding her remaining earring to the light, about how precious it must have been to her, and nothing has ever looked more delicious to me in my life.

Nothing deters me from dropping the jewelry into my mouth—not the looping metal nor the inevitable bacteria. I open wide and savor the flavor of pennies. I run my tongue through the blob of feathers and blood and imagine the woman's face leering at me through the car window, aghast, maybe hurling her fists at the glass. This earring was important to someone. Now it's mine forever.

Swallowing the thing proves more inconvenient than I anticipated. I jab my chin with my wounded fist and feel a pop as my mandible dislocates, but the earring hook drags against my esophagus so that I'm sure my insides looked like a car with keyed side panels. I gulp like a fish, trying to open wide enough for the earring to find its way into my stomach and stop causing so much trouble. Bile surges up my throat in retaliation, but I swallow it down, the earring flowing with the acid back toward my gut.

A coughing fit overwhelms me. My body is angry with me. It wants to hurl the invasive metal back out. Extrude it like a cancer, but it doesn't. I keep the jewelry down and the vomit where it belongs.

Progress!

Just as I start my car, Cris bangs on the window. "My rate is fifty dollars an hour. Call me when you book our next show."

Chapter 12

Lola is fast asleep by the time I return, although she left her door cracked open instead of locking it shut. I'm tempted to peek inside her room to check on her, but I resist, instead heading to my bathroom to clean up.

My reflection in the bathroom mirror is so gruesome that the very sight drains the evening's high straight from my pores. It oozes out of me. Whatever symbiote latched onto my brainstem to birth Disco Mama seeps away. She leaves behind the regular, wasted, pale-skinned me of before. I wear the blood of her hunt on my face and in the gash I chewed into my own hand. My skin pulses at the edges of the sore as my frantic blood cells rouse the troops to stitch the mess back together, but other than her left-overs, nothing of Disco Mama remains. I am me, and once again, I am revolting. I've got blood smeared all over my face, under my jaw, and clotting in the widow's peak of my hairline. Everywhere I've scratched, wiped, or itched since I bit myself is stained with blood. Flaky red saliva cakes in the corners of my mouth, and my mouthwash congeals into a purple sludge when I rinse. My throat stings from the earring, which is still caught somewhere in my chest as my body works fruitlessly to drag it into my stomach. Breathing hurts as torn flesh meets oxygen for the first time. My mouth tastes of copper and puke.

My phone buzzes for the tenth time since I've been home and I hurl it through the door, across my bedroom. It lands on the wooden floor like a brick and then it is quiet. I don't care who it is, but I especially can't bring myself to speak to Jimothy right now. He'll know just by my breathing that something is wrong. He always knows. Now that he's gone away, his calming influence on this family no longer reigns supreme.

My husband loves to be helpful, to an annoying degree. The act of it fills his tank, just gasses him the fuck up for weeks. Perhaps I hate it because the weight of my disarray seems to swing heavier on my shoulders with each of his accomplishments, mainly his ability to capture the heart of my daughter while she's always maintained a healthy distance from me. I suppose it stands to reason she would love the same kind of man that I do, but there's a connection between them that grates on me. There's only distance between the two of us, mother and daughter. Just like me with my mother.

The moment 25-year-old me saw my positive pregnancy test, I promised myself I would be nothing like my mother. Perhaps not better, but different, which illustrates the bitter savagery of mothering. While we meticulously inspect our psyches like chimps picking out the lice of our own parents' betrayals, we fail to see the brand new kind of monsters our mothers molded us into. We may think we have agency, but we're just blind fish at the bottoms of miserable caves dug for us in utero. Still, I really believed *I* would be better. It wouldn't even be all that hard to be better than her. That woman was like math, a construct loosely defined, understood only by the theories of all the people in her orbit.

The only thing my mom said when I told her I was pregnant was, "I thought I taught you better than that." This was news to me, who was under the impression all this time that she hadn't taught me anything. I expected her to laugh in my face, call me foolish, and explain in no uncertain terms that she intended to be as "devoted" a grandmother to Lola as she had been a "mother" to me. Instead, she dropped her disappointment into my lap, turned on her heels, and left the room. Just *left*. The unplanned pregnancy didn't bother her so much as my stupidity. I sat there holding a picture of my first sonogram; at the time, I'd convinced myself it was an epic *fuck you* to my mother. I planned to stick the grainy image on her refrigerator as a reminder of her poor influence on my life, as if the mistakes I was making were articulate threats instead of the pathetic mewling of a young woman begging for someone to love her.

She walked out. My brick shithouse exterior was fortified even further by her casual dismissal. I decided then that I would never try to show her a single picture of my baby ever again. She would never meet my Lola, my child.

For all her apathy and drunken, faraway stares, that inscrutable bitch never cut me off completely. Then she died before the grandchild I privately hoped would bring us together could even be born.

As an adult, and despite any of my assertions otherwise, I know that I am not a person who manages, but the one who needs managing. My mother understood this, which is why she kept quiet and observed me without interference as I wandered aimlessly between axes, swimming in thoughts of my own independence, belief in my self-restraint, and my ability to take perfect care of myself. I was a double-negative daughter, rebuking all labels of the positive. Her voice was never my guide; her absence was, and whether by accident or design, it was the only guidance I'd ever have respected.

Jimothy understands this too, always has. He knows from experience how to identify a walking crisis when he sees one. If Lola was to have a fighting chance, she needed a person like Jimothy in her life. That much had become clear in the few years we spent together without him. I would never bring the kind of stability he would.

These are the things I think about as I sanitize and bandage the hand that I chewed through like a teething puppy. I am flushed and blushed and ready for bed when I hear a thump.

"Lola?"

The insulation in this house has molted inside the walls, in the way of old newspaper. If my daughter is awake, she'll have heard me.

"Lola, are you awake?"

Nothing. Silence curdles the room as every manner of crime show narration plays in my head. *The man was murdering Regina's daughter as she cleaned her face, the negligent mother having left her child unattended all that Friday night. She was completely unaware of the killer's presence until the lifeless body of her child dropped to the floor. The murderer slipped on his own kill, alerting the mother just down the hall. Frantic at the thought of being caught, the murderer tossed the daughter's body aside, slipped out the door, and caught the mother by the neck as she went to check on the odd noises coming from her daughter's room.*

In fiction, this is precisely the moment when a character's blood would run cold, but mine doesn't. I'm hot again, in the menopausal sense. My entire being is radiating sweat and anxiety. I am lit up and I'll stay that way until my circuits fry or I see the rise and fall of my sleeping child's chest. Even then, I might not calm down for a few hours.

I'm in Lola's doorway without remembering the walk, only to find an empty bed. This is when the ice forms. Terror roots me to the floor until my eyes focus in the dark and settle upon Lola snoring softly on the floor.

"Fuck me," I say. I can't help it. She hasn't rolled out of bed since she was eight years old.

My voice–not her sudden plummet to the floor moments before–is what startles her awake. She jolts upright, accusations half-formed before she's even opened her eyes. She speaks in slurred sleep speak that I understand to mean, *what the fuck are you doing in my room?*

I answer her by offering a hand. "You rolled off the bed."

Barely conscious, she accepts my help, only to recoil at the touch of my sloppy, gauzed up wound.

"What happened to your hand?" she asks. Nothing quicker than worry to drag a person out of their dreams.

"I'm fine. Just a cut. Get back to bed."

But she yanks me by the wrist, studying the damage like a personal injury lawyer. "Tell me what happened, Mom. I mean it."

"Lola, I'm tired. I cut my hand and I'm too cheap to go to the doctor. So I used your dad's emergency kit."

At this, she smiles. "I'm going to tell him."

"Do it and you're grounded forever."

"This looks really bad, though."

"It feels bad, too. Go back to bed. I'm tired."

Lola drops my wrist and gazes absently at my hand for a few seconds before crawling back into bed. "How did you know I'd fallen out of bed?"

"I heard a thump. Didn't it hurt?"

"Not really. I was asleep."

I start to lift my hands in mock offense but think better of it. "Next time, I won't bother you."

"No, Mom. It's okay." Moonlight hits her sharp features perfectly. She is so beautiful. I can't recall ever looking at my mother the way she is looking at me now. Maybe I haven't done as bad a job as I think.

Then comes the switch. All the warmth on her face disappears and everything clicks into place–her understanding that she might be more responsible than her own mother. I can feel it. A mother knows her child, knows their voice, their stares, and their smiles. Even a bad mother knows them, perhaps neglects them, but even she knows them, just as I know Lola.

I close her door until it clicks, the unshakeable shadow of the moment burrowing deeper into my guts with every step I take back to my own end of the hall.

❂ ❂ ❂

I start out the next day hustling the counter clerk at the phone store to have my bricked phone replaced under warranty, all while maintaining as pleasant a demeanor (by which I mean, bordering on hateful) as I can muster in the face of a twenty-year-old who must jerk off to the Verizon terms and conditions statement every night.

"The corner looks a little mangled," he says. His name tag reads, *Hi, I'm Kenneth.* Of course, his name is Kenneth.

"Normal wear-and-tear, Kenneth."

"I'll have to ask my manager."

"Sounds like a great idea, Kenny. Please *do* fetch the manager."

Common sense dictates better manners, and infantilizing a person never begets positive results, but I am tired, my throat hurts, my hand hurts, and I've waited in the corner of this sad, grey store—a store allergic to benches in any form—for two hours. Now, Kenneth is resisting my demands. At least a manager has the authority to give bitchy customers what they want, and believe me, I intend to be a huge bitch. I'm vibrating with attitude. I can tell Kenneth senses it by the way he flicks his gaze toward me in quick little bursts, uneasy about maintaining the impenetrable eye contact I level at him. He has baby smooth skin, our Kenneth. Dark thoughts unzip my lips into a nasty grin. I can only imagine the balm such infant skin would be against my tattered throat.

But, alas, the manager arrives, shoos Kenneth to the side, and assertively tents her hands on the counter. "How can I help you, ma'am?"

She looks about my age, years of customer service gouging the skin around her mouth. This is a woman used to frowning. Her name is Suzanne. I can tell already that I have lost.

She's pointing towards a display before I can even ask how much a new phone costs.

Suzanne gives me a terrible deal on a new phone. Eight hundred dollars later, I am out the door. It comes with a ruby-red case and free (free!) glass coverage for six months. Their best price, if you ask Kenneth.

I've got fifteen missed texts and four voicemails when I activate my network. About a third of them are from Jimothy. (I asked Lola to text him about my broken phone, but it appears she forgot.) I see a few from Cris, and the rest are from a number I don't recognize.

Sending my husband a courtesy "I'm alive" text, all my attention then diverts to the strange number.

Hello Disco Mama. My name is Marcus and I used to work with Cris's uncle. She told me about your show last night and I'm wondering if you'd like to play at my club this Friday?

I've got an open spot. Will pay. Call me back if interested.

I've left you a voicemail as well.

Disregard if not your thing.

I don't bother with the voicemail and immediately text Cris back.

WHO IS MARCUS

I know him, he's cool

He owns a club?

Until a few weeks ago, I hadn't stepped foot in a club for decades. Now I'm being courted by them. What a fucking trip.

He works for one, books talent.

What club?

Marcus, the club promoter, responds quickly to my questions when I text, but I decide to confer with Cris before confirming anything. The club is named CLA$$H, yes, with two dollar signs. I've never heard of it. Sounds stupid. Reviews sit firmly in the two-to-three-star range, but I don't give that much consideration. Only a nerd would bother leaving a bad Yelp review for a nightclub, and I don't much care what a pack of silly nerds think. Not like they'll be in attendance after my on-stage savagery.

The whole place smelled like puke.

Bartenders are rude.

Had to wait in line for re-entry.

Yup, sounds like a club.

Just then, my phone rings. It's Jimothy.

"How's your mother?" I ask upon answering, hoping to deflect any prying into my own night-time doings.

"The same, I guess, which is worse. What happened to your phone?"

"I dropped it in the toilet again."

"You need to stop putting your phone in your back pocket. What is this, your third?"

Fourth, but that's not relevant. "Everything is fine over here."

"It seems that way. Lola hasn't texted me to complain nearly at all."

"Hasn't she?"

"Only the first few days. After that, it's been normal. 'Hi Dad' and 'school was fine.' Seems you two are managing alright."

"Sure we are. It's not the same without you, though."

"That's funny," he says, his chuckle dying on his lips as soon as it escapes. "That's the one thing Lola keeps repeating when I ask her."

"Are you surprised? She's always been a daddy's girl."

The silence on the other end lasts a beat too long, the precursor to a delivery of bad news.

"So, my brother is coming up to Mom's," he says. "Little."

We never refer to his brothers by name, it's always Middle or Little. Middle is generally an easygoing guy, not much to make waves or demand much. Little is a tornado: chaos, hilarious at parties but torture to debate with, due to his unwavering and near-constant assertion of his correctness. Little's arrival adds time to everything, from family dinners, to holidays, to meetings regarding the division of parental assets. He doesn't mean any harm; he's just annoying.

"So your stay is further extended," I say.

"Yes, most likely."

"You know, once he gets there, you can probably leave. Let him act as a proxy or something."

Jimothy would never do this. *Never.* To even suggest it reduces his odds of coming home by at least another twenty percent. His brothers blame him for making their mom crazy, because he married me and inherited Lola. Marilyn's demand for that paternity test was the one thing that woman could have insisted upon that Jimothy would deny. He didn't want to know the answer, and it tore them all apart. Spectacularly.

"You know I can't," he says.

"Then tell him not to come."

"You know I can't do that, either," he says.

"Then what do you want me to say?"

"Nothing. I guess I don't want you to say anything."

"Look, I'm sorry. You know I suck at this."

He pauses on the other end before continuing. "I wish you would try to listen. At least sometimes."

My immediate defense mechanism to statements such as his is to point out all the ways he has let me down in the past, but he ends the call before I can get there. He cited "mom needing him" as the excuse.

That went well.

I should feel bad about how the call went with Jimothy, but I don't. I should stay home this Friday and watch a movie with my child, but I won't. The shoulds and woulds always seem to land on my shoulders, boxing me into a life I don't recall ever wanting. Then again, I never considered what kind of adult I wanted to be when I was younger. The idea of adulthood never registered beyond the incorporeal ether that was my future. Who's to say this isn't exactly where I'm supposed to be?

Lola sits at the kitchen table with her head in her hands, sniffling and rose-cheeked from crying. All my misgivings from moments before evaporate into an indiscriminate rage at the thought of someone harming my child.

Flinching at first at my touch, Lola relents and allows me to hold her.

"What happened?" I ask.

"He called me," she says, wiping her nose on the inside of her shirt.

"Who? Your dad?"

"No."

For the life of me, I can't envision another man in her life with enough sway to elicit such a response, and I'm folding the previous days, nights, and weeks in my head, until the origami crane of realization hits me in the face.

"You kept talking to that drummer boy."

She says nothing, which means yes. Once again, the prickly cool of a *should* settles onto my spine, because I should be furious with her disobedience. Believe me, I am furious, fucking radiant with it, and the source of my fury lives inside my wallet in the form of that full-grown man's dumb smirking face on his dumb fucking driver's license.

I ask her what he said to upset her. The way her body tenses in response chills the room.

"Nothing. It's nothing. I'm never speaking to him again."

"Tell me what he said. I won't get mad at you."

"You, mad at *me*?" Her hands drop to the table with a smack. "After what you did?"

"What I did? I just got home!"

Lola springs up and away from me, sending the kitchen chair screeching into my feet. "He told me what you did that night. You ate his driver's license. You said you were going to shit it out. He told everyone that you're insane. People keep asking if I'm as crazy as you. They look at me and whisper."

"They who?"

"Kids, Mom, everyone at school. Emily told everyone."

Emily. That little twat. If she was standing in front of me, I would smack Emily's pretty little face until my palm print was as good as ink. My fists are white just thinking about it. I never did like that girl.

"She sounds like a whore of a friend, Lola."

"She's my best friend and now she looks at me like I have shit on my face. What did you do to him?"

Lola's face is a bleeding wound and I want to run my fingers under her trembling chin. I want to apologize for losing my cool and ruining her friendship with the worst teenager she could ever choose as a friend, but ruining it, nonetheless. I want to explain to her in a way she would understand: that I acted out of fury and love, fury because of love, its indignant tendril unspooling from my bowels where I'd hidden it all these years, a constrictor around the injustices of my own youth now freed by the primitivity of motherhood.

"Is he telling the truth?" She's crying again, hot tears nearly evaporating from her brilliant, red cheeks.

I open my mouth and lie straight to my fragile daughter's face.

"He's a liar and a moron, Lola. I'm not proud of my behavior that night, but he's trying to break things, break *you*, to show how strong he is. It's what weak men do when a woman dares see too deeply into their psyche. So, no, I did not eat his driver's license. That's absurd. I did slap the shit out of him and make his lip bleed, though."

Her shoulders soften, but only a little. She doesn't believe me yet. "Why do you still have his license?"

"I wanted to see for myself how old he was, and he handed it over. I just didn't give it back."

"And the blood?"

"Split lip."

Lola's scrutiny burns my skin, but I refuse to flinch. Honestly, I'm quite impressed with how easily my lie weaves together. If I spin it just right, Lola might have a chance at turning the tables at school. Held under the lens of common sense, which story sounds more truthful? One must simply ask the gossipers if they're stupid enough to believe such outlandish tales. Lola can force their reconsideration. A high schooler will sooner eat their own arm off the bone before appearing stupid to their friends.

Lola calms down enough to sit back in her chair. If I hadn't broken her trust already with my odd hours and suspicious behavior, I'd have her totally convinced.

"Everyone is already talking about it," she says. "Emily is being so weird."

"Everyone is weird in high school. Even you, I'm afraid."

"People think you're a freak, which means I'm a freak."

I place my hand on top of hers, testing her anger. She doesn't move away.

"Honey, if anyone actually thought this story was true, they wouldn't dare make fun of you. Otherwise, I might show up to school and eat their math book or something. All the best stories are outrageous, and how much more outrageous can you get than me eating some asshole's license? Give it a week. Maybe two. Someone will get knocked up or caught smoking meth in the teacher's lounge and this will all be old news."

Lola levels her big, brown eyes with mine. "And if it doesn't?"

"It isn't a question of *if.* People are infuriatingly pre-dictable. Believe me when I say you are one cafeteria fight away from total irrelevance."

Thankfully, she accepts this for now, but still spends the rest of the day sealed in her room. For my part, I root myself to the kitchen table and plot. No matter how many times I relax my hands, two white-knuckle fists reappear within minutes. My body can't relax with my mind swirling into the toilet the way it is. I imagine myself showing up to Emily's house on a stormy night, knocking on her window from the dark, and holding her car keys over my open mouth. I imagine what I'll hiss at her. *Mess with Lola again and I'll eat your entire car. I'll eat your shoes with your feet inside them. I'll swallow you whole and shit you out in pieces.* I can almost smell her fear, a cold sweat like the sweetest perfume. Her body would flail back onto her bed as I shove her by the face and send her ass-over-heels and not let her up until she seriously considers her future.

But I can't do any of these things. Lola still relies on Emily's friendship, whether I like it or not; with her, I must play nice for my child's sake. For now.

The drummer, on the other hand.

I'm such a goose. Calvin Lehr is fair game, and I happen to know where he lives.

Fate, God, or what-have-you, has a way of stepping in just when you need it. I've never prayed my thanks more sincerely than the moment I plugged Calvin's address into Google Maps only to discover he lives a mere ten minutes away. Looks like my evening just filled up.

I've got no plan, only bad intentions. Before I leave, I make sure to knock on Lola's door to deliver my alibi.

"I'm going to run to the grocery store and get some snacks. You want anything?"

Initially, she responds with silence, but my phone trills with a message before I'm even at the bottom of the stairs.

King size twix and an iced latte <3 thx mom

"Glad to be of service!"

Lola makes no further indication of hearing me, and soon I'm puttering merrily down the street in my Kia, playlist on low volume, listening intently to my GPS's monotone directions as I head just past the grocery store towards the drummer's house. The drummer lives a few songs away. I instantly recognize the neighborhood I'm going to. Like most cities, my hometown has a wrong side of the tracks, and that's where Calvin lives. The thrill of my mission makes my face numb, but not in the shameful way I feel when I eat Lola's old pictures. Instead, it's orgasmic. Everything is hot. Everything.

The freeway dissects the landscape a mile or so beyond the overpriced marketplace where I shop for Lola's pre-bottled lattes. The houses start to hunch over on sagging patio beams until the second story disappears from the track housing design completely. There are no HOAs here to keep the weeds in line, and most of the houses haven't been painted since they were built. Still, there are lovely, mature ficus trees lining the roads and front stoops littered with kids' bicycles that give the area a homey charm my own is missing. Jimothy and I chose our home right after the wedding. We were young and thought the clean yards were a sign of hospitality and comfort. Only now do I realize the yards are uncluttered under threat, and most of my neighbors keep their vile personalities caged up in their garages in the form of barely-legal porn, Bud Light, and Trump flags. Or, in my case, bloody drivers' licenses.

The drummer's house sits at the end of the street, and I pull around the corner and stop near the communal mailbox. This way, anyone noticing my car will think I'm either a resident getting my mail, or a guest of any of the five or so homes situated near the graveled space in which I've parked. Plus, the drummer would have no chance of spotting me from a window.

Car in park, I sit in the driver's seat and realize I haven't planned anything beyond getting here. I can't just knock on the door–how anticlimactic. What if Calvin's got some kind of doorbell camera? Last thing I need is video proof of my insanity going viral throughout Lola's school. I need to be smart. Careful.

It strikes me that the drummer could not even live here anymore. He doesn't seem like the type to keep on top of responsible things, such as updating government institutions with his address change. I'll have to hedge my bets and hope I'm right. I can't stay here forever, watching. Someone will eventually see me, and I have zero good and honest reasons to be here.

Just looking at Calvin's house flips some internal switch, and the anxiety of moments before suddenly seems asinine. Who cares if Calvin sees me. In fact, I want him to. It reminds me of a nature show I watched once, where an orca tail-whipped a stingray five feet out of the water before circling back to eat it. I'm that orca. I need to send a message. I want this man to know that I know where he lives, that I know he is trying to gut my kid's reputation, and that he is a ridiculous loser with nothing better to do than prey on kids and then pick on them until they're suicidal. A voice screams at me from the remaining pieces of my rational self–the voice of Jimothy, my Jimothy Cricket. The message plucks on my spine–*be good, stop this, you are crossing a dangerous threshold*–but my darker impulse, those monstrous unraveling tendrils, have seen too much sunlight. They will not be quiet now.

Today, I'll start small. See how it plays out.

As a mom who never plans ahead for any occasions and usually finds myself wrapping gifts and signing cards in the driveway before events, I keep scotch tape, a pen, and kid-friendly scissors in my glove box at all times. Today, that tendency to procrastination pays off. I tape the drummer's license to the front of the mailbox (number 4) using the entirety of the roll, to make sure it doesn't fall off. The delight of imagining Calvin's face upon discovering my little gift entertains me the entire ride to the marketplace, through the aisles, into the self-checkout with Lola's Twix and latte, and all the way back home where Lola is waiting at the bottom of the staircase.

"What took so long?" she asks.

On the other side of the freeway, I imagine the drummer has just stopped at his mailbox on his return home from his part-time job at a movie theater. He remains frozen on the sidewalk for many minutes before tearing the scotch tape apart like a possum just to hurl his license across the street in disgust. He will retrieve later, but only with gloved hands. Until then, his body ices with discomfort. He feels eyes all over his body.

If I were a sane woman, this is where I might stop.

Chapter 13

It's midday, just after lunch, and the interior at CLA$$H evokes a liminal feel, a not-quite-rightness that prickles oddly on my skin. All the lights are on, but the well-lit space's emptiness makes it seem cavernous and spooky. Daylight pours through the porthole windows on the main doors, catching one of the chrome table tops in its spotlight. Clubs are supposed to be seedy, dirty, a little fringe, sweaty, slick with skin and bad choices; seeing a venue like this is like seeing Grandma without her wig for the first time. Because of this, I'm struggling to envision my performance here. I just can't *see* it, can't feel it, even though Cris and I ran through a couple of ideas over text.

CLA$$H is a definite upgrade from the Rat House. Though I feel a pang of wistfulness in moving on, the feeling fades entirely once I see the party arsenal now at my disposal. Marcus leads me and Cris through the electronics, asking what kind of set we're working with. He seems confused when Cris answers him instead of me. And while I feel more like an imposter today than at any other point in my life, I try my best to reek of pretention–I'd rather be thought of as an elitist than an idiot. Cris (she's a quick one, no wonder I like her) redirects Marcus by asking about payment. He offers an offensively low number that summons a contemptuous huff from the hollows of Cris's chest. Marcus beckons her around the corner where I catch the fiery tips of their whispers, although I can't make out the conversation beyond that.

CLA$$H is where people expect to dance all night. It's a place where people snort meth in line out front. The crowd will also be extremely drunk, but unlike the booze-centered Rat House, this place is serving uppers in the bathroom next to the tampon dispensers. Chairs aren't optional: they're illegal. In just a few days, I'll be nose-to-nose with a sea of overlarge pupils, and I better make sure to deliver.

I'm wondering if this is what it feels like to care about a job and quelling the simultaneous churn of dread and elation in my gut when Cris whips back into sight, obviously upset.

"This is fucking bullshit," she says.

"Couldn't agree on a fee?" I ask.

"There is nothing to agree to. It was all set up."

"What does that mean?"

The tears come then, despite her best efforts to stop them. "My uncle set it up."

"Is he some kind of DJ Godfather or some shit? What do you mean he set it up?"

"I mean he paid Marcus to let us show here. We get whatever my uncle donated."

Ah, I see. Cris, young, naïve, little Cris is under the impression she and I scored this gig because of our miraculous charisma and talent; that Marcus, somehow having heard of our spectacular feat at the Rat House, was so enamored he swept his schedule clean and shoehorned the new big thing into the first open slot.

My first impulse is to wax poetic about meritocracy and tell Cris what giant crocks of shit men are. I could give a whole lecture on how music industry dudes only put in real work when they're trying to exclude rather than promote talent, but I need this girl-child to be in top form this Friday. What she needs right now is a hype man, not a lesson. "So what? We're in, right?"

"That's not the point–"

I hold my hand to her lips, gently pressing them closed before she annoys me even further. "It is entirely the point. How do you think anyone gets anywhere? Talent? Fuck that. I got into the Rat House because I haunted the owner like a slimy poltergeist. I refused rejection, and after I made an ass out of myself, I made him let me come back. None of that was due to talent. That was a series of right-place-right-time events and being a pushy bitch. You and I have been handed the beautiful gift of exposure, and you want to stomp on it because it was *given* to you? Believe me, Cris, people mutilate themselves for this kind of opportunity. Don't let your ego spoil a good thing."

Cris doesn't speak, but I can tell by her ferociously crossed arms that she isn't sold yet.

I continue, "Think of it this way. Your uncle believes in you so much that he has invested his own pocket money into this adventure. I don't know about you, but if I had an uncle like that I would think twice before spitting in his face."

I've got her. She drops a hand to her hip and sighs. "If you say so."

What a good girl. Now that this issue is resolved, I can return to event planning in my head. "We've got some changes to make."

❁ ❁ ❁

Cris and I spend the next few days in constant contact: speaking on the phone, texting, and emailing. I threw some big ideas at her after leaving the club. I envision cascading lights on cue with certain transitions, Warhol-esque videography, and a confetti dump that puts New Year's Eve to shame. Things too big for our budget. While Cris initially hesitated, she eventually jumped in headfirst, even recruiting one of her friends to consult on videography and screen casting. There simply isn't time or money or crew to do everything I asked for, but what Cris accomplishes in mere hours is impressive. I'd really love to introduce her to Lola–Cris might be just the type of friend she needs. But I digress.

The show at CLA$$H is tomorrow night, and unlike my other two performances, the nerves have not yet caught up to me. I am shockingly unworried, which should worry me, but I figure I'll put my eerie calm to good use while I can. Tonight, I'm making lasagna for Lola and me. It's the way we like it–no meat.

Surprisingly, Lola hovers in the kitchen, shredding cheese and fetching pans when needed. She does this silently. No gabbing about her day, no gossip, and no questions, until the lasagna is safely in the oven. Only then does she lean into me like a newly minted FBI agent.

"What is going on with you?"

"What do you mean?" I say.

She's picking at her cuticles, a nervous tic that irritates me to no end. Why would someone do that to such pretty nails? Then I look at my own, remember my mother harping about the whorish orange of my nail polish, and decide to let it go.

"You're never here. Where do you go?" she asks.

I'm not sure how to respond, so I don't. Lola takes this as an admission. She presses me. "Are you cheating?"

All the breath leaves my body at once. I'm not angry; more mystified by my daughter's profound misunderstanding.

"Who is Cris?" she asks.

I laugh, and laugh, then laugh some more. That dirty little sneak. "'Cris' is short for 'Cristina.' Unless I've become a lesbian and didn't know it, I'm most assuredly not cheating."

"Then *who* are they?"

I've been wringing a potholder in my hands, and I slap it onto the counter for effect. This nosy child is going to blow my cover before I'm ready. Disco Mama can't be hidden forever, but her reveal to the family will be my doing, not hers. I need to distract Lola off the scent. "Every child goes through this eventually. I'd just hoped it would take you a little longer. I should have known better. You are my kid, after all."

"What does that mean?"

I'm nose deep in the freezer now, searching for the bottle of vodka I bought after visiting Calvin's mailbox. "It means that, one day, you'll discover that your parents are fallible, stupid humans who do stupid things."

"So, you *did* cheat?"

"No, goddamn it. But I did lie. I do lie. Often." If I know my daughter like I think I do, she will absorb everything after this pronouncement of guilt like a greedy sponge.

"Who have you lied to?" Her face is already contorting with hurt. The sight of her pain over something as silly as lying makes me want to scream. Thank God for vodka.

"Get a grip, child," I say while fetching two shot glasses. Time to teach this child about her heritage. Better now with me, than getting blackout drunk around Calvin and his ilk. Besides, a buzz will stop this interrogation immediately.

"Emily's dad will be there the entire time!" I mock.

She flushes but finds her resolve quickly. "That's different."

"Look, Lola." I slide the Jessica Rabbit shot glass toward her. "You're smart, and we can debate all night about the arbitrary rules of acceptable and unacceptable lies, but I am tired. I would love it if you could just take your drink and ponder this shit by yourself for a while. Everyone lies. We lie daily. Sometimes we act guilty about it, as if truth is the singular measure of goodness. Sometimes we do it simply to make our lives easier. Sometimes we do it because we are being total shitheads. But we *all* lie, and we all tell every form of lie. The only way you win in this life is being better at it than everyone else in the room."

Lola stares at the vodka I present to her.

"This isn't some kind of test," I say. "Drink it, or don't."

Finally, she says, "I don't know how."

"It's a drink. You drink it."

"Last time..."

I should have known she wouldn't have waited for me to taste the sweet nectar of liquor. She knows who she is without me. Jimothy can try all he wants, but she's *me*, through and through. I'm more impressed with her secrecy and sheer audacity than alarmed by her behavior. The irony smacks me in the face. I should have known; I was just like *my* mother, too. I guess there are some things a person just can't change.

"What about it? You choked? It burned?"

The worry drains from her face, and she laughs. Maybe the irony hit her, too. There's no need to play coy about alcohol when your mother is pouring you shots. Luckily, we still have some root beer in the fridge.

"You need a chaser," I say. "Don't breathe. Drain the shot, then take a swig of root beer. If you do it right, you'll hardly taste the booze."

Lola brings the glass to eye level, spilling a bit over the edge. Then she drinks it down in one gulp, coughing before reaching for her root beer chaser.

I rub her shoulder and put the vodka away. "You'll learn."

"I tasted everything."

"How do you feel?"

Wiping tears from her eyes, she says, "Warm, and it stings."

I wrap my arms around her shoulders. "Just like a good lie."

❂ ❂ ❂

My ruse works like a charm. I hear Lola giggling in her room upstairs for thirty minutes post-shot before she falls asleep. One shot and she's down for the count. I suppose I should be relieved that she's not already as good a drinker as I was at that age.

Now that the coast is clear, I depart to my bedroom with my headphones and laptop, ready to run through the setlist for tomorrow. Incoming texts on my phone ding on the regular. There are a few from Jimothy, whose mother escaped her care facility. I told him to sue them for negligence. Another one is from the activewear company I bought running shorts (which I use for pajamas) from two years ago and never bothered to unsubscribe from their marketing materials, and about fifty from Cris. Thank God I addressed the relationship to Lola before she caught sight of this wall of word vomit from my secret partner.

The texts are borderline ramblings, but, essentially, Cristina is freaking out.

You run through the list? NO CHANGES!!!! I've spent twelve hours programming strobes and you will NOT fuck this up last minute

What time will you be there

I'm setting up at 3. They're closed but Marcus will let me in

Don't tell my uncle about this

I message back that the cat is already out of the bag with her uncle, but she is quick to respond.

I might have borrowed some stuff. Don't say anything

She talks as if her uncle and I are in some secret cabal of old people whispering to one another between bites of oatmeal. Cris can't possibly fathom how little I care about her uncle's opinion of me, let alone his opinion of her. I care about the performance. I care that Cris can pull her weight because I can't do what she does.

It's only a show, Cris. A performance. No one is dying. You aren't going to be arrested. Your uncle signed off on this already because he wants you to be happy. He won't care that you got a little sticky-fingered to ensure you made him proud.

Now, I like Cris. She's clever and resourceful and knows what she wants. I don't think she'd maliciously tank the show, but she's young enough to surprise me. I'll burn down her cousin-uncle's store if she goes off-script. Only *I* am allowed to fuck things up.

You do your job and I'll do mine. CLA$$H will have no idea what hit them once we're done.

The house is quiet. Cris mercifully ceases messaging me. Upstairs, Lola is passed out and I have the rest of the night to myself. My headphones pinch my ears, so I remove them, taking the music to a low volume as it runs its course. I'm not sure what I'm looking for in the set. It's practically perfect. Starts low and grumbling with a rhythmic bass that makes my muscles twitch. There are a few cuts to classic metal, but I never allow the entire chorus to play before transitioning into a new track, something the audience will have likely never heard before. Cris and her friend have the visuals locked in, with a few little last-minute extras I've asked for.

I catch myself daydreaming instead of paying attention, which is the only cue I need to realize there is nothing left to do but hurry up and wait for the show. Sleep will not be happening for me tonight, so instead of fighting it, I wander into the kitchen to look for snacks, maybe a protein drink to keep me satiated until morning. There's a jitter in my fingers that refuses to abate, a tremble like a caffeine overdose, and I know nothing will calm me.

Despite what I keep telling myself, this show must go off without a hitch. It must succeed, or else I've blown up my entire life for nothing.

A peculiar sensation overwhelms me somewhere between slamming the fridge shut and opening the pantry, and I freeze. My ancient lizard brain is trying to communicate with my dumber modern self, and a warning stands the hairs on my arms on edge.

"Lola?" I call, but she does not respond. It couldn't have been her anyway. The presence of my child would never alert me so wickedly.

My phone reads 12:15 a.m. I suppose I was listening to music longer than I thought. The house is quiet. No messages, no emails. All the lights are off, aside from the kitchen recesses, and a shiver slimes its way over my skin. Something is wrong, and I need to figure out what it is.

Like all proper suburbanites, my first instinct is to glare through the peephole of the front door. Surely the perpetrator will be standing there nefarious-like, knife in one hand and bag with a dollar sign in the other. Instead, the view is ordinary. My plantless pots, where I keep the pinecones I collect from the neighbors' trees, remain intact and undisturbed. My car sleeps peacefully in the driveway. There is nothing to see–until there is. A flicker, a shadow of something darts between the Kia and the garage door before slipping out of view.

I watch a little longer but don't see any more movement. Nothing further indicates an intruder, yet my skin ripples with goosebumps. There will be no resting until I go out there and check for myself. Luckily, this is a scenario I've played out in my head many times over the years, a character trait bred into me after years of living feral and mingling with other broke addicts. I quietly fish through the kitchen cabinets for the cast iron skillet.

Sliding on the soft outdoor slippers I keep by the back door, I strain to hear beyond the throb of blood surging through my temples. There is nothing. Holding my breath, I slide the back door open, praising Jimothy from afar for his neurotic attention to dirty door jambs. The glass door closes with a hush.

Moonlight oozes onto the simple desert-scaping of our backyard, leaving me cloaked in the shadow of our patio awning. It's chillier than I expected and my fingers ache from squeezing the pan so tightly. I stay frozen on the patio for a few long minutes, feeling a mix of anxiety and indignance that makes my stomach feel like it's full of spiders. Then, I catch the crunching sound of footfalls on the gravel on the other side of the house. There is someone here, someone confident enough to sneak around my yard with impunity.

Adrenaline does funny things to a person. I tremble and sweat profusely under pressure, but sometimes my senses congeal into a single laser beam, an all-encompassing focus that snuffs out any fear of injury and inflames my primal need to exterminate the threat. It's like that time a neighbor's dog charged at me while I was getting my mail. A slow-motion serenity consumed me as I mentally played out my options: kick it in the throat, jab my mail key into its eyes, choke it with its own collar. It never came to that, because the mutt skidded to a stop before it reached me, my neighbor collecting his animal before things could progress.

I suppose this is the fight part of flight-or-fight, which comes in handy as I tiptoe around the side of the house. I realize I've forgotten my phone inside, but I still have the cast iron pan.

The closer I creep toward the side gate that separates the front and back yards, the clearer the sound of whispering becomes. I pause to listen only to discern that there is only one person present—not two, thankfully. They like to talk to themself. The words are indistinct, but the tone is clipped and breathy and angry. They sound like a man, and something about the voice registers as if I've heard it before.

My foot slips while trying to peek over the top of the gate, and the sound of displaced gravel stops the muttering briefly before resuming. They rustle through a bag. The next sound is unmistakable: I'd recognize the tinny clink of spray paint anywhere, both because I was somewhat of a wild anarchist in my youth, and because I have rehabilitated far too many yard sale finds in my adult life, which all wound up in a dumpster due to extreme ugliness.

This must be a kid. Is it one of Lola's friends or a boy she's rebuffed? Or maybe Emily and her mangy boyfriend, trying to twist the blade they've already plunged into Lola's back? This realization switches off my stealth mode and thrusts me into a rage. I burst through the gate screaming for this person to get the fuck off my property, not even looking at their face until they stumble backwards, ass in the gravel, throwing their hands in front of them in surrender.

I succeed in scaring the shit out of this twerp, but the moment I see his stupid smarmy face, I stop screaming and start to cackle. "Spray paint? You really *are* a dumb child, aren't you."

Calvin jumps to his feet, embarrassed again by his terminal lack of machismo.

"I know you came to my house," he says.

The weight of the skillet tears at my biceps but I don't dare release it. "Stay away from my daughter and all of this ends."

"I want nothing to do with your slut daughter."

He's either blind to the skillet in my hands or too arrogant to think I'll use it, because those are some bold words. I shoot back, "Don't make this get ugly. Go home and don't come back."

When we were dating, Jimothy taught me to never turn my back on anyone, especially a man. It's a lesson he learned after being mugged at a Taco Bell. I made this dangerous mistake at the gas station a few weeks ago, and I will not repeat it.

Calvin reaches for his bag, but I tut aggressively. "Leave the paint."

"I paid for it."

"A fact that doesn't change if you leave it behind."

"I'm taking my stuff, you bitch." The drummer snatches his bag before I can intervene and turns to leave. "Like mother, like daughter," he says, and though his back is turned I can visualize his smirk as he says it, as if he's won something, him and his backpack filled with paint.

His parting words are meant as epithets: mother and daughter, both dumb, bitchy whores. He is satisfied with himself. Then, this silly man turns his back to me. In his mind, I am not a threat. He is the exact type of man that refuses practical advice until it hits him in the face. Lucky for him, I am happy to oblige.

He doesn't see me coming, just keeps walking as I sneak closer. Just as I'm close enough to reach out and grab him, he turns and I whack him in the temple with the skillet with every ounce of my strength.

The iron drops him right there in the driveway, and I lean over him as he wheezes, his eyes rolling to white. I set the skillet gently near his head. A trickle of blood leaks from his ears before haloing the edge of the pan.

"What I say, goes. And I said that the fucking paint stays here."

Chapter 14

The reason mobsters chop people up in bathtubs before disposing of their corpse is logistics. I don't have the luxury of time. I need Calvin's body off my lawn before the neighbors see something they shouldn't, so I back my car out of the garage and use its bulk to block the crime scene from view. Then, I race inside for a fitted bed sheet and lay it next to his unconscious form.

Moving a limp body is difficult. First trick is to rotate the hips in the direction you want them to roll, so I sit down, grabbing him by the wrist with one hand and the ankle with the other, brace my feet along his mid-section, and pull. It takes a few tries–he may be a twerp, but he's still got the body of a man–but I eventually get him propped onto his side. After that, all I need to do is deliver a precise and powerful kick from the other direction so that he falls onto his stomach. All that's left is tucking him into the sheet, bracing my feet on the cement, and dragging his dead weight with all my might until we reach the security of the garage.

I back my car out of the driveway, park on the street, close the garage door, and leave Calvin on the floor to sleep it off. Then, I spray the blood trail of his injury into the gutter with a garden hose. It's one in the morning and suspiciously quiet. I feel as if the entire neighborhood watches my sins from their windows, voices hushed and holding their breath. More than once, I bend the hose to stop the flow, thinking I've heard a voice or the beeping of a phone dialing the police. Silliness, of course; this is nonsense. My mind is completely fried.

Now, there is the issue of what to do with him. Let him go and he'll squeal. Keep him here and he'll try to fight me or call the cops or both. An ambiguous plan begins to form, like spotting a darting shadow in my peripherals. What I need to do is let it simmer on the backburner and trust that it will expose itself. No better way to facilitate that process than to return to my show planning. After verifying the drummer's still-unconscious state, I grab my laptop and seat myself on the garage floor. I try to ignore the odd noises escaping his body as his brain attempts to jumpstart him back to consciousness.

"If you insist on interrupting me, you can at least listen to my set."

The drummer makes a gurgling noise and his lips twitch. Curious, I run my fingers over his rough, unshaved cheeks. The feel of him is repulsive, oily, and unkempt; his skin is prickly, and I imagine it catching every stray bacterium and mote of dirt in the unfortunate vicinity of his face.

I'm reminded of the vastness between Calvin and Kenneth, the boy at the phone store: oily, sure, but still vivacious and pink-cheeked with soft, apricot skin. Kenneth will soon become a man like the one laying before me; a realization that inflames me all over again as I imagine him rubbing his infected face against my beautiful child.

I kick the drummer in the jaw for good measure, but the sound is dulled by my spongy sandals. All he does is drool and moan. I try to return to the run-through at hand, but his noises are distracting.

"I'm really going to need you to be quiet," I say. Is he even conscious enough to process my demand? His fingers are twitching. The twitching is bothersome. All this sudden movement pulls me away from my work.

My shadow falls on him as I leer at him, crouching over him like my own drunk mother, unable to fit her giant turkey into the oven at Thanksgiving. Calvin's eyes flutter open, but when he catches me staring he immediately shuts them again.

Kneeling next to him, I gently boop the tip of his nose. "Hello in there. Can you hear me? Can you move?"

"What happened?"

"Do you know where you are?"

"I..." The strain of coherence wrinkles his forehead. "Who are you?"

How lovely would it be if I knocked him into another self? A concussion of major proportions, a mind eraser. Maybe I can send him on his way with a brain injury and no one would ever be any wiser. An accident. He was drunk. Hit by a car. Got in a fight. Mugged.

My wonder doesn't last. Just seconds after asking who I am, recognition dawns over his features, and the theatre curtain rises to expose the entire plot. The drummer instantly begins to scream.

I smother his mouth with both hands. "Wake up Lola and I'll stab a screwdriver through your temple."

He quiets, but his heart, oh his heart, it thrums with terror, and I smile.

"You're pretty fucked up, my guy. I clocked you good. Probably concussed. Maybe a fracture or a brain bleed. Who knows? That skillet is fucking heavy. If you stay quiet, I'll drive you to the hospital. Say a word about any of this and I'll find your mother and slit her throat. You hear me? I will fuck up your entire family, which I tried to warn you about back at the Rat House. One could argue that you brought this on yourself."

His lips try to move under my hand. He is trying to respond.

"I won't say anything," he wheezes. I probably damaged his neck, too. Oh well.

The drummer manages to prop himself to a sitting position, with a little help. His lower jaw hangs slack and he's drooling. The sight of him is so repulsive I must spit all the mucus in my mouth onto his feet just to get it out of me, as if just his image was enough to infect my salivary glands like a virus.

"Think you can walk?" I ask.

He tries, but his strength fails him. He scoots as close to the wall as possible. I hold my index finger to my lips and raise the garage door. I need to move the Kia closer so I can shove him into the back seat.

The frightened alertness of just moments ago has already faded. He could pass out again at any moment, so he better get in the fucking car before he does.

"Get in the car and I'll take you to the ER."

Helping him to his feet is the closest I ever want to be to this man, but I simply don't have the energy to drag him all the way. I need him to help me haul his body into the car. His knees buckle after a few steps, and his freefall takes me down with him. Luckily, I fall on top of him instead of the other way around. He doesn't move, so I try to bring the car closer to him and inadvertently run over his hand in the process.

He screams, and I scream back. "Get the fuck in this car or I'll do it again!"

This works. He thrashes like a human still getting used to having legs, but he does it. He is finally in the back seat of the car and off of my property. No one seems to have seen or heard anything, and we are gone, whoosh, out of sight and flying down the empty freeway.

Behind me, Calvin is quiet. He wheezes and coughs occasionally, but he's quiet. I'm pretty sure he's passed out again when his limbs suddenly seize with renewed recognition.

"What happened?" he asks.

"You were trying to tag my house–Lola's house. You remember her, yes? Well, you climbed onto the block fence with your spray paint and slipped. Landed right on your head."

I watch through the rearview mirror as he rubs the wound on his head. "I don't remember that."

"Knocked yourself out cold."

"Where are we going?" he asks again.

I turn the radio on until I find 94.9 FM, Arizona's favorite classical station. Hopefully, this will help calm him down.

"We are going to the hospital," I say, and for a brief minute I wonder if that's where I should really take him. He's delirious and suggestable. He is so concussed he likely couldn't remember the details if he tried, and even if he did, who on Earth would believe him? The severity of his injuries precludes clarity. He might have foggy bits of it, but never the entire picture. Even then, who could prove maliciousness? No one. I was a mother, home alone at night without her husband, with a child to protect and alerted to the strange noises of a midnight intruder. I even brought the fool to the hospital. It's self-defense. Easy.

I must have intuited that I was teetering on a precipice. The hospital idea was a lure to get him into the car. He might not remember anything, but then again, he might. He might talk. The cops might come to the house. They might use luminol or whatever neon shit they have to see the shadows of his blood. They could see the drag marks into the garage. That's not the work of a frightened mom, but of a murderer hiding the evidence of their crime.

I drive and drive, fleeing the city via the I-10 exit by exit until there are miles between off-ramps. The drummer stargazes from the back seat, his bloody forehead stamping the rear window red. He's transitioned from asking what has happened to him to needling me every two minutes about where we're going. Each of my answers etches away at his trust in me. The lights of the city become dimmer and dimmer, until they are gone and the only light to puncture the dark comes from the high beams of an occasional semi. Not even a concussion dulls his primal drive to survive, and I'm not surprised when he starts to yell from the backseat.

"Where are we? Where am I? Where are you taking me?"

In an instant the drummer's confusion mutates into fear, which grants him the strength he sorely lacked earlier. He goes feral, kicking the seats and desperately pulling on the door handles. For a minute I lament the safety features of the modern car, because Calvin hurling himself from a moving car would solve a lot of my problems. I resort to screaming at him again.

"Stop kicking my seat, you fucking dipshit! Goddamnit!"

The wheel jerks as I turn in my seat to yell at him, and we fishtail across three lanes, but I'm able to regain control before the car crashes into the divider. Even then, he's still yelling, pounding on the window and demanding I let him out. I could—we are deep enough into the desert that he likely would never find his way home, considering his injuries. But no, I have to see this through. I'll feel better knowing exactly where he is at all times, anyway.

The drummer does not relent. He pounds so fiercely on the window I fear he'll break it, which is precisely when I bring out the big guns—my mom voice.

"Sit the fuck down and shut up or I'll drive this car into the wall. Don't think I won't!"

Blessedly, he obeys.

"I'm not going to take you to some hospital in town. It's got to be further out, where nobody knows you. They'll figure it out eventually when you come to your senses, and then you can go home."

"Just take me home," he pleads. "Take me home."

"No," I say, and the drummer begins to sob. Huge streams of tears and snot cascade down his face. This is an intolerable development. Of course, he *would* find a way to evoke pity, even from someone like me.

By the time we reach the next exit, the drummer is inconsolable. I take the nearest exit, Roadrunner Street, following the unlit side road. There are no signs of life, nothing but the shell of an abandoned gas station. It's here, in a place lit only by moonlight and the cool blue lights of my dash, where I finally stop.

The drummer hushes his wailing. He blinks away tears as he tries to discern where I've brought him.

Locking eyes through my rearview mirror, he ceases crying completely as pieces of his memory knit together and I can tell he understands just how much shit he's in.

"I'll leave her alone," he says. "I won't say a word, I swear. Not about tonight and not about Lola. I swear to God."

The drummer's voice is eerily calm, and I wonder if he's in shock. He might try to fight or even sprint into the desert if I startle him.

"Look," I say, only now twisting my body to face him. "Now that you seem lucid, can I ask you a question?"

He nods slowly. His pupils don't match but he is listening.

"Why Lola? And don't feed me bullshit. You are a man who seeks out children. They're nothing but naïve targets to you. What was the point?"

My spine is as rigid as a coat rack. The drummer sucks on his lips, hopefully thinking deeply about his response. His hesitance elicits a furious heat in my cheeks, making me wish I'd brought the pan with me. My palms are sweating. Nothing exists beyond this moment but the thrum of my own heart and the occasional whoosh of the freeway, which is when I realize I've asked the unanswerable question. Calvin can't possibly deliver any response that will soothe me. All I've done is needle him until he'll say what I want to hear, which is that he's a pervert dirtbag and my pursuits this evening are justified and necessary.

"Actually, never mind. Let's get you out of here, alright?"

He's not going anywhere, though. He was never going to leave this car alive. It took me this long to understand that myself. As I exit the Kia and round the car to the back hatch, I hear the drummer ask again what has happened to him. My teeth itch at the question. He is so annoying, and it bugs me that Lola's foolishness helped get us here. That girl refuses to listen to her mother.

Speaking of my daughter, she always makes fun of me for keeping a wad of plastic grocery bags in my trunk. I've told her that this is just something moms do: we save bags from the store and teeth from our kids until we die, and our descendants must pick through the trash of our lives.

I'm turning out the bags in search of the few without any noticeable holes when Calvin attempts an escape. He jerks the door handles violently, but is still too injured and confused to figure out how to unlock them.

"Put your seatbelt on," I say. "Then I'll take you home."

He's fiddling with the seatbelt, unable to latch it without losing his grip and his patience, so I return to his side of the car, slide into the seat next to him, and smile as if I am there to help him. The way his glassy eyes gaze up at me, pleading for help, to be taken home, momentarily stalls my hands. The pair of us freeze together, locked in time, a diorama worthy of Edgar Allan Poe, savoring the last seconds before our lives as we know them effectively end.

Calvin leans away from me as I grab his seatbelt, but relaxes to the zippery sound as the belt is dragged over his chest. "You have to pull it out further. Give yourself some wiggle room."

The buckle snaps into place, and before Calvin realizes what I'm really up to I've got a plastic bag over his face and the rest of the slack-hanging polyester looped around his neck, and I'm pulling as hard as I can as he bucks in the backseat, and I climb on top of him, my elbow pressed into his jugular, the seatbelt irritating the cut on my hand until my new skin rips open and there's blood everywhere, and goddamn he's strong, but I'm determined, and I squeeze and squeeze and squeeze some more because strangling someone is fucking difficult.

I'm not out of breath–I'm not breathing at all. I'm a bag of flesh and muscle. The drummer tries to chew through the plastic bag over his head but he's getting weaker. He shreds the skin on his neck trying to pry the seatbelt loose, but he can't, and I've got him boxed in just right with the belt and my body, and he's not fighting quite as much, and then he's fighting less, and my body trembles from exertion, and the seat belt slips a bit because of all my blood, but I catch it and I squeeze all the way down to the black little center of myself.

And then I breathe, swallowing the air around me in gulps. The drummer is still but his pulse still bellows inside his body, his final, silent plea to live, until I'm squeezing for no reason because the pulse is gone, and so is Calvin the drummer.

I'm reluctant to release the seatbelt, although I do let it loosen as my muscles finally succumb to exhaustion. One of Calvin's fingers remains wedged within his noose from when he tried to pry himself free, making his final moments a pathetic tableau.

No more wet, wheezing noises, no more questions, no more pleading, and it's eerie at first before a sensual pleasure sweeps over me. Silence is one of those things you don't ever fully appreciate until you're run over by the solitude of it. It's just me now, just me and this sack of flesh who used to cause me so much frustration. Relief seeps out of my pores. He'll never bother me or Lola again. Silence. Perfection. I have never been more at ease.

The drummer is still warm. The slack way his lips hang from his mouth betrays the serenity of the moment. Moonlight floods through the open door and casts a gentle spotlight onto what I have done. I have to say that Calvin has never looked better. He died the way he lived: wailing like a fucking baby. There's purity in his final moments of terror and I find that deeply appealing, and I stroke his cheek, no longer repulsed by the oils and grime that adhere to my fingertips. He is just a little boy now, like all men are little boys. I am struck by a nostalgia of emotions. Calvin is someone's son, but when I conjure thoughts of his mother, I'm met with revulsion rather than regret. What a shit job she did with this boy. Just look at stupid little Calvin.

An itch tugs at the back of my brain and I can't force it out. Could be some kind of Pavlov's conditioning on account of where we are. Something about the gas station, a seedy and dirty place that draws me to perform my most audacious acts. Or maybe I'm hungry. Starving, really. I am positively famished.

Climbing over the body, I drag Calvin out of the car by his ankles. It's not nearly as difficult as before, and I have no issue laying him mangled in the dirt. I am driven by another impulse now, one that overrides all others. I must feed.

As I loom over him, small drops of saliva drip onto his shirt. I'm drooling, and there is no stopping me now. One swift punch to the chin to unhinge my jaw, and I crouch to my knees to finish what I've started.

The same mind-numbing calm sweeps over me as I surrender myself to the whims of my basest cravings. The scent of him drives me wild. The bones in my shoulders pop and I open up wide for my meal, starting at the head so that the arms stay pinned to his side on the way down, no elbows sticking into my ribcage, and I can't breathe as I'm stuffing his head into my mouth, so strange a feeling having this heap of human stretch and tear my gullet, but now that the process has begun, it can't stop. I can't stop. Getting past his shoulders is tough, and I struggle for a while, laying on my side in the dirt with a corpse spilling out of my mouth. I just open up like a constrictor, take my time, and trust my beautiful body to do its work. It knows what to do, just like it knows how to breathe, birth, and shit. My mouth is a gaping black hole, and it stays wide even as the drummer's feet pass through my windpipe. I won't close my mouth for hours. I might never close it, a forever sucking abyss always anticipating a meal.

Then, I am alone again. Just me, the spidery-torn flesh of my bulging torso, and a breeze whistling through corroded plywood and lonely paloverde trees.

Chapter 15

After my feast, I am more ready for tonight than I've ever been. The mound of my stomach catches on the steering wheel, but I manage to wrench myself out of the driver's seat anyway and stagger to my feet in CLA$$H's parking lot. I don't remember much about the drive–I didn't then, and I don't now. All I know is, one minute I was regurgitating a sneaker on the shoulder of the freeway, and the next, it was dusk and I was watching a line form outside the front doors of CLA$$H.

I can't find my phone, which means I likely have dozens of texts from an anxious Cris. I don't care. I am grounded by debilitating fullness. It's the sense of engorgement that spins the human body into panic, makes it shut itself down so the human doesn't keep listening to their appetite and eat themself to death. Despite this too-full feeling, I am peaceful. The stage-fright agitation and nerves I felt before earlier shows fails to appear. I practically glide towards the back entrance, one hand gripping my antlers, and the other my show bag. I walk in at seven forty-five. The show starts at nine and I'd promised to arrive no later than six.

Every molecule of serenity I bring to the building, Cris crushes tenfold with anxiety. She is cursing by the time she sees me waddle to the stage.

"Where the fuck have you been?" she says.

"Calm down. You think I'd miss this?"

"You were supposed to be here two hours ago. You weren't answering your phone. Wait–what happened to you?"

She's locked her eyes onto my torso. Horror seeps into her features.

"I lost my phone."

"Your stomach."

"I have IBS." Offering nothing else, I allow Cris enough time to manifest her own explanation. The trick with lying is to be confident in your bluntness. Offer too little and there is nothing left to cover the lie; offer too much, and it's too easy to dissect. Leave an assertive crumb and the human brain weaves its own understanding.

Do you know nothing of irritable bowel syndrome, Cris? How lucky for you.

"I don't move around much anyway. I'll be fine," I say.

"Are you sure?"

I drop my bag with my mask on the stage, and approach to place an arm around Cris. "It's going to be great. I promise. We'll wipe that shit-eating grin off Marcus's face. Just you watch."

The crease in her forehead relaxes. "I don't want to mess this up."

"You won't," I say. "I'm going to change, and then we can go over all the new tricks you cooked up."

So. Here's how it goes.

Cris runs me through the basics. I pay just enough attention to get the job done, but my mind is somewhere else. I have the technology to speak to the crowd now—not with my voice, but with my keyboard. I wanted to communicate with the crowd without interrupting the music. They've got a scrolling marquee just above my head, ready to blast whichever message I choose. This is perfect.

Cris is thorough as always, and by the time she's confident with our setup, I know what I am doing and we are very close to show time. We both tap into the susurration of the crowd forming just outside, hoping their energy will guide us through the set. Every yip and holler from outside erodes my nerves. Some of the patrons already sound drunk. They want a show—good. I want to give them one.

"Are you ready?" Cris asks.

I nod my head, but I'm slipping away into a fog, and it's dark now, so dark. I am nothing but a fleshy bag of neurons and meat. I disassociate. Now I can see everything.

I crane my head to the moon and then back to my hands, dripping with blood. I can't breathe now; something blocks my esophagus, but I don't panic. It's just right. Everything is perfect. The drummer's scent orbits the mound of him he's made my belly, and it's night and it's dark and my fingertips jolt the board when I touch it. My body churns and ripples as I sway. Then, I'm on stage. Cris is gone. A sea of shining eyes greets me. Fog spews out from the machines just off stage. And I type as a slow, bellowing soprano roars into the room. My voice. Disco Mama's voice.

WE ARE GOING TO START SLOW

My operatic entrance does not impress the audience. As they boo, the drummer shudders as he dissolves a little more in a sluice of my stomach acid.

I WILL NOT TOLERATE DISOBEDIENCE

They jeer again, louder. I love this discordant song, truly I do. The background chorus of the track kicks in and we are getting close.

DISCO MAMA DEMANDS QUIET NOW

They do not obey. They scream.

QUIET CHILDREN

My music vibrates the floor. I know Cris is ready in the wings. Almost time now. Almost. The vocalist of the song mellows, as if on my command. The accompanying acoustic guitar crackles like an old radio and the song fissures into something new.

BE QUIET
I WILL BLOW YOUR FUCKING HEADS OFF

Now the vocals explode into a vicious scream, carrying with them the mightiest of all electric guitar riffs, and the crowd in front of me wails with delight as I damage their hearing for life. Cris's light show sears blood red lights into their retinas, and even the drummer in my belly stills because the moment is fucking iconic.

These people, every single one of them, are under my command. Their rapt attention lassos me in place; to leave the stage would be to drag them all with me. The faces in front of me mutate into an insectoid kaleidoscope—shiny eyes all squished into one amorphous creature, and I direct them where and how to move, how to flail their limbs in dance, and they obey.

One song after the other, the crowd swoons. No one breaks away; they are a tight little den of debauchery. I've gotten better, too. Thanks to Cris and her training sessions, I know how to clip songs, repeat beats, save them on deck and find them when I need them. Cris has her job dialed in beautifully. The girl truly might have a great career in this.

The bartenders inhale tips like insatiable cash herbivores, but only between beat changes. You have to give the dancers moments to breathe, or else they tire and leave. I let them cool enough between songs to grab more fuel and return to me. When it's time to prepare for my departure, I bring coolness into the room again. The drummer stirs my belly, my body fighting to digest him. No matter—I'll prevail, but the heft of him sends labor-like shocks around the band of my belly. My lower back screams just like he did when he awoke on the floor of my garage, like he did when I wrapped the seatbelt around his neck. No matter. No matter at all.

A variant of grief fills the empty spaces inside my head as the music dims. I like it loud enough that the noise stops my thinking, but the opera lulls the room to a stop in the way only a powerfully loud woman can do, and I can only think of vertical-pupiled men, of snakes, of the cold dark night and the crack of my jaw and the horrible yet intoxicating taste of the drummer's greasy hair as I shoved his head down my throat. Nothing like the gentle dissolve of baby Lola's paper and wax drawings, but so much more filling.

The edge of the stage crystallizes as the music ends, and I finally look at the crowd, truly *look* at them. The lack of noise centers me in the worst way. The audience is screaming, they are thrilled. Someone points at me and shouts drunken gibberish, which is enough to awaken my feet and force me to flee the stage. I enjoy their adulation, but only from a safe distance. God help us all if they try to speak to me.

Once safely backstage, I tear my mask off, repulsed at how it bounces off the bulge of my stomach on its descent to the floor. I am huge. Grotesque. Inhuman.

A compulsion greater than any I've ever felt shreds my nerves as the events of the last few days collide into my psyche all at once.

Look at me. What have I done? My jaw is on fire. Just moving it to breathe blasts pain from my temples to my collarbone. The swell of adrenaline fueling my past twenty-four hours finally sputters out, and my brain doesn't know what to do with me now. Things were fine when my body took over. Bringing my brain into the mix makes me feel like jumping from a bridge. The hormonal plummet brings me to tears, which is a release I didn't know I needed. In this moment, I think of Jimothy. For the first time since he left, I actually miss him. I need to call him. I need to call him *right now.*

"I'm panicking," I tell myself as I panic, as I tear backstage apart looking for my bag. "I'm fucking panicking." I repeat the mantra to soothe myself, to make it less corporeal and more just a stress response, but sometimes intuition hits like clairvoyance. After searching fruitlessly backstage, I find my phone hidden under the driver's seat of the Kia. The screen is riddled with missed calls and texts. Fuck. Fuck, fuck, fuck.

Not wasting my time reading the novel sent in clipped bursts to my phone, I make my first call to Lola. "What's wrong," I ask.

"Dad is looking for you. Where are you, anyway? He seems pissed, Mom, like really pissed. Are you at a club?"

"I'm fine. What did he say?"

"What is that music?"

"What did he say, Lola?"

She pauses. "I think Grandma died."

Fuck. Fuck that horrendous woman.

"Shit. Do you know when?"

"No, he wouldn't say. Just kept calling because he couldn't reach you. Then he got mad."

A hand lands on my shoulder like a vice.

"Cris, *fuck*, what are you doing?"

She says, "I'm sorry! Wait, are you crying?"

Lola's muffled voice, jammed against my ear, sounds like she's being smothered with a pillow. "Mom, what happened? Mom? Who are you talking to?"

"My mother-in-law died, Cris. I really need a minute."

Cris throws up her arms and mouths an apology. However, she does not leave.

"Is Dad coming home?" I ask Lola. This is my worst nightmare. As much as I'm missing him, Jimothy can't come home now. He just can't.

"I don't know."

"I'll call him, I guess." Lola keeps peppering me with questions about where I am and what I am doing, and I have no choice but to repeat that I will explain everything when I get home, and she needs to get off the call and let me call her dad. Finally, she relents and hangs up.

Cris pipes up immediately. "I don't want to intrude, but you ran out of there like you had shit your pants. They won't invite us back if you spew diarrhea all over the floor."

"That's real cute, Cris."

"I'm just trying to lighten the mood."

"Thank you for that. Can I please deal with my family now?" I'm restraining my temper as much as possible, but my true voice seeps through anyway. Cris doesn't recoil exactly, but her eyes flash wide and immediately narrow to form an expression I'm quite used to seeing in people who get too close to me. A new malicious sensation takes hold as she leaves. Will I ever stop systematically destroying every relationship in my life?

The phone rings. It's Jimothy. I answer without pleasantries. "What's wrong?"

"Where are you?"

"Where are *you*? Lola said your mom died?"

"Don't flip the script. I have been trying to call you for hours."

"What is going on with your mom?"

"Why won't you answer my question?"

"Because I don't care to be interrogated. You called me, so why don't you just tell me whatever you wanted to tell me. Or did you just call to lecture me like I'm your employee? Or worse yet, your child?"

Jimothy does not respond to this. He doesn't respond at all and being the bitch I am, I refuse to offer any further commentary. He can ask if I'm still there. He can be the olive branch. But after a minute he still does not speak, which is incredibly disturbing until I catch the faintest whisper of a sob, as if he's holding the phone away from his mouth so he can freely cry. His softness will always puncture my stony veneer. Maybe it's because he rarely lets go—before today, I've caught him crying only twice in our entire marriage. He's the caretaker. Needing care is an unfamiliar feeling sensation for him, far more distressing than any death. And I suppose those rare moments of vulnerability prove how much I rely on him to keep me grounded. His crying only exposes my own weaknesses; his absence rips away my shiny, white veneer of false sanity.

His response shrivels my insides so profusely I might prove Cris right and shit out the drummer's corpse, right there in the parking lot.

He says, "You know you can't hide anything from me."

"What is that supposed to mean?"

Jimothy lets out another mewling sob. "You know, I'm out here taking care of my mother, away from home, missing you guys, and you can't even bother to take my calls. Lola tells me you leave all the time. I sent flowers to your work, by the way."

The mention of work immediately unwinds the knot in my chest. "So that's what this is about."

"My mom died," he says, no longer hiding the emotions curdling within him. It all comes out with surprising ferocity. It's enough to blow my hair back. Marilyn was a wretch, but she was still his mom and he will mourn her like all children mourn their mothers—both the reality of them and the fantasy which, now, never will be.

"When did you quit your job?" he asks, tone turning on a dime. The man is truly losing it.

"Does it matter?"

"You don't seem to think so."

"I didn't want to stress you out even more. You've been one bad day away from a mental breakdown for weeks."

"You know what? Do whatever you want. I'll let you explain things to Lola when we can't pay the mortgage." And he hangs up. That motherfucker hangs up, just like that. Grief seems to have stuck hatpins into the pink flesh of his brain, because he has never hung up on anyone before in his life.

The urge to hurl my phone is quelled only by the sound of someone clearing their throat behind me. It's Cris, and she's been watching the entire time.

A rumble erodes my insides as my poisonous thoughts leach into my stomach. I can feel the contraction as my body goes to work. The heartburn knocking at my tonsils abates instantly, and I smile at Cris. She crosses her arms and says, "You are psychotic, you know that?"

I grin. "I think I might do something different for a change. I'm going to listen to my husband and do whatever the fuck I want. Do you know what I want, Cris?"

"No, what?"

"Come with me," I say, pointing towards the neon strobes of the still raging club. "We have another show to plan."

Chapter 16

Lola is bereft when I return home, her face puffy and red from crying. One look at my stomach freezes those tears.

"What happened?" She points to my midsection. I am cartoonishly round. The skin looks ripe to tear.

"IBS and stress. It's happened before. I'm fine."

"Did you lose your job?"

I don't know if I should be distressed or impressed that Jimothy told her. Usually sabotaging our child's psyche to win an argument is *my* tactic.

Without getting close enough for Lola to graze against my swollen stomach, I guide her to the kitchen and plop her into a chair while I start some drip coffee. It's eleven at night, but I think we each could use a little kick.

"First of all, I quit my job. I didn't get fired. Second, your dad is having a hard time up there. He's been taking care of Grandma, with whom he already has a strained relationship. Now she's died and he's..."

I catch myself staring at the coffee maker as I consider my next words. "I suppose he's unmoored. Happens to the best of us, even your dad. He's still human."

"If you quit your job, where have you been going all the time?"

Jimothy likes to act like a saint, but he's just as petty as the rest of us. Lola never mentioned a thing about my extracurricular activities until her phone call with her father.

Lola rises before I can come up with an answer. She says, "Never mind. You'll just lie to me anyway. You already told me how easy it is for you to lie."

The indignity of her behavior, however warranted, brings out my sharp side. First Jimothy hangs up on me, and now this. I snap, "Sit down right now and listen to me."

For once in our relationship, she listens to my buckshot directives. I glide to the chair opposite her, our kitchen table now a neutral zone between mother and daughter.

"I don't owe you any kind of explanation because I am the parent, and you are the child. This might make me a bad mother, but the truth is never kind, now is it? I don't owe you an answer, I am giving you information because I want to. Lord knows I can't keep having you and your dad trading intelligence behind my back as if I'm some mole in the family. And he sure as hell won't listen to me after today. However, he might still listen to you."

I'm hoping that if I tell her everything she'll buy into the secrecy of it, hold it sacred like a jewel only we can touch, and stop conspiring against me with Jimothy. She stares intently, her face not betraying a thing. I smile. She has been paying attention. I've never seen her so hard-lined and stoic. She's just like me.

"I quit my job because it sucked, and I didn't feel like doing it anymore. Instead, I've become Disco Mama."

Lola's reaction, while subtle, reads all over her face. She thinks I'm crazy.

"What does that mean?"

"I'm a DJ."

"No, you're not." Leaning back in her chair, she crosses her arms as defense against what she perceives as another lie.

"My first show was at the Rat House, actually."

"No, it wasn't."

"Yes, it was."

She still doesn't believe me, but my stone-cold frankness is starting to affect her. "Why?"

I'm careful with my answer. I want her to feel in cahoots, not terrified of my systematic unraveling of her normal suburban life. "You might say I was bored."

"That doesn't make sense."

But it does make sense. All of it makes sense. I was annoyed with my sneaky daughter, annoyed with myself for allowing it, annoyed at Jimothy's departure in favor of his she-beast mother, annoyed with the drummer thrusting his greasy dick toward Lola from the stage, annoyed at how supremely terrible his stupid band was. My skin was itchy with irritation that demanded fixing. I needed to conquer something, and music is what I chose.

"One day, you'll understand. There's no point getting into that now."

Lola presses her fingers into her skin until the flesh whitens. I don't break the silence.

"So," she says after a few empty minutes. "Does this mean I can come to one of your shows?"

"You're seventeen, so probably not. Most clubs aren't as loosey-goosey about fake IDs as the Rat House."

"The door guy is in love with Emily."

"Speaking of Emily," I say, annoyed once more to be reminded of that snaky little slut. "I think you should invite her over. Maybe next weekend. What do you think?"

"Why?"

"For dinner. I take it she's still being weird about this whole drummer thing?"

My stomach audibly gurgles in response to the mention of Calvin, and I wonder how much of him remains inside of me. Breathing has become easier over the past few hours and my heartburn has declined. The human body is a spectacular creation of nature–even as it is digested.

"She's actually kind of mad at him now. Says he ghosted them the other night and won't return her boyfriend's texts. She asked me if I've heard from him."

"Have you?"

"No. But I blocked him anyway."

Good girl. "Invite Emily over."

Lola nods slowly, hesitant.

"Set that up. I'll deal with your father. He's going to be fine, though. Don't worry. Just give him a nice hug when he gets home. And don't breathe a word to him about what I've told you tonight. He won't understand, and I'd hate to realize that I can't trust my own daughter."

With that, I rise from the table and leave, making sure to pat her gently on the shoulder as I pass. At best, I've bought myself a few days. Lola won't talk tonight–but she will, eventually. Her loyalty has never lain with me.

Safely in my room, I listen for her familiar thudding steps as she heads off to bed, and only then do I flop into my mattress. This is the first moment in days, maybe longer, that I've allowed myself a moment to relax, and my body responds with vicious contractions as the drummer wreaks his vengeance.

I place my hands over my belly to calm him, like I did when I was pregnant with Lola. Just like back then, I am both amazed and repulsed at how my body adjusts to such internal trauma. The normally loose pouch of skin sheltering my pelvis is taut with the swell of my last meal. Angry, red stretchmarks orbit my belly button, a patterned chaos resembling shattered glass. My body is hot to the touch as it fights this invader. The pain sears like torn tendons in every possible direction. To move is to ache, to snap, to bleed, and my pulsing hand leaves a slimy blood print behind as I push myself up from the bed. I hadn't noticed my freshly rebleeding hand until now and wonder if that's what Lola was asking about as she pointed to me in horror from the doorway. Every motherly gesture this evening must have marked her with blood.

I find myself collapsing in front of the toilet, also much like I did when I was pregnant. My body can't tell if it wants to retch or shit or both, so I place my cheek to the cool tile floor and let nature do its work.

The only indication that I'd fallen asleep was the freefall sensation jerking me awake. The bedroom lights are off, which is odd because I remember them being on as I waddled to the bathroom. Shadows swim in the darkness as my vision fireworks itself to consciousness, and it's a little too quiet in the house. The ache in my stomach abates enough for me to climb to my feet, hands squared on either side of the powder room for purchase. I feel light, almost empty, like I could float through walls, like I'm nothing.

I see the drummer in my mind's eye. I feel him inside my gut. He's punishing me from the inside out, making me relive it. He'll terrorize me until I release him.

In my mind, I scream at him to get the fuck out of me. He is so stupid, but all of this could have been avoided if he'd had an ounce of sense. *Just run, you stupid prick*, but he does not hear me–because I am not awake. I am trapped in this lucid dream of Calvin's conjuring, and I cover my own ear as the pan smacks into his stupid, useless skull, as I drag him into my garage, as I gaze around to search for onlookers, as I hide from myself, as I see the change in my eyes, so vibrantly yellow with dripping red lines for pupils. It's Disco Mama's face.

And then a splitting cramp jars my eyes open to the sallow yellow light of my bathroom. I'm face down on the tile as the drummer emerges from my body. My throat shreds like Christmas ribbon as his remains splinter my insides on the way back up.

I purge him in globs, red and stringy meat punctuated with shards of bone, a rib here and there, and specks of rubber from the second sneaker I managed to swallow. It's a smorgasbord of entrails and bile until Calvin's head rears up. His skull dams the red waters of my throat and I feel the acids backing up behind it, and gasses fill the newly emptied spaces in my body. I can't breathe, this stupid big-headed fuck is going to kill me even after he's dead. Men like him truly are an unshakeable scourge, but even if I asphyxiate here and now on the skull of this dumbass, I will be content, because at least he's dead too.

Time slows as lack of air sends my brain into a tailspin. I think of Lola finding me on the floor in the morning, bloated and blue and rotting; imagine Jimothy flying home to hold her, just to remark at my funeral that he knew he never should have left us alone. The pinprick of annoyance that image conjures is enough for me to evacuate what remains of Calvin from my stomach into the toilet. Then, he's out and I'm gasping. I'm broken and sore and oxygen-deprived, but I'm not dead, and that cursed skull clunks onto the tile dripping with bile and blood and saliva. I drool pink on the floor and collapse.

It takes daylight for me to peel myself into a sitting position. The toilet struggles to swallow my monumental purge and finally clogs after ten attempts, which means I need the plunger. Judging by the coppery light coming through the bathroom window, it must be early morning. There is little risk of Lola being awake to see me in this state, but I must be careful.

So, I shower, closing the curtain on the Jackson Pollock-looking massacre as I scrub myself clean. Not even scalding water rinses the filth from me, but it will have to do. I wrap my towel around my torso, unstick the skull from the floor, and gaze into its empty sockets. There used to be a brain here, eyes and lips and acne and attitude. Now look at it. Just bone. Humans truly are nothing of consequence.

A part of me wants to smash the skull on the floor, but that will only make another mess for me to clean. I think I might keep it. It came out of me; doesn't that make it mine, anyway?

When the skull is rinsed and safely stored in my closet, I fetch the plunger and begin my morning task of methodically forcing bits of the drummer down the toilet until every piece of him is gone. It takes an hour, plus extra time to mop, scrub, and bleach the walls and floors, but the effort is worth it–not a trace of gore remains.

By the time I'm sitting at the kitchen table with my coffee, it's only eight in the morning, and what a delightful day it is. Despite nearly dying, the morning could not have gone any better. You never realize how refreshing a deep breath can be until you truly choke on something.

My phone remains eerily quiet, meaning I've managed to make Jimothy murderously angry. He'll cool down in a day or so, and in the meantime, I'll enjoy the small sliver of peace before the catastrophe of his imminent return. "Catastrophe" might not be a sufficient enough word. When Jimothy comes home and sees with his own eyes what I've become, he might force my hand into an act far more cataclysmic than offing a nobody-drummer-loser. I just don't have the energy to think about that now.

Lola trudges downstairs around ten and wastes no time interrogating me once again.

"Did Dad call this morning?"

I hold up the dark screen of my phone as an answer.

"He's not texting me back," she says.

"He's dealing with a lot of logistics right now. He'll reach out when he has time. You dad always makes time for you." Normally, this is a sentiment laced with jealousy, but today I feel nothing at all. My ravaged body can't handle any more trauma at the moment, so my brain floods me into submission with gigantic waves of serotonin.

"Did you say something to him?"

"You know, it's not always my fault whenever your dad does something wacky." Yes, it is.

"What if he's flying home? Does he seriously not know about the DJ stuff?"

"He seriously does not know, and if he did, he'd have been home a long time ago." The thought of him walking through the door has me grinding my molars.

Lola stops and glares at my midsection. "You look better."

"Feel better too."

"So, it really was IBS?"

"Why must you question everything I say?"

"Because everything you say is questionable, Mom. You never make any sense."

"No?"

"No, Mom, I don't think that's it. I mean...a DJ? Of all things."

Becoming Disco Mama should be the least confusing aspect of my personality. Venom foams behind my teeth and I swallow it back before spewing it onto my daughter, because she should know better, my child should know me better than this. But then again, how well did I know my own mother before she left and died?

"I'd think you'd be happy to finally have your father home." My tone is pure acid.

Lola sits across from me and sighs. "Normally I would, but you're both getting so weird now. He can't come home to you like this. He'll flip."

"We'll manage. We always do."

"Do you?"

I quell another temper flare as I realize Lola is not making accusations. She's confessing.

"What are you really trying to tell me?"

Sinking into her chair, she covers her eyes with her hair and looks at her feet. Guilt congeals the air so ferociously I fear globs of it might dislodge from its orbit around my head and break a window.

"I promise I won't get angry. Please tell me what has upset you so badly."

The quiet picking noise of Lola tearing at her fingernails is the only sound for some minutes. It's enough time for her to change her mind.

"It's nothing," she says. "Honestly. I'm just worried about Dad."

Taking pains to appear calm, I sip my coffee and shrug. "Whatever you say. I'll be here if you want to actually talk."

Lola nods and heads back to her room, and though I can't be sure, I swear I hear her mutter under her breath as she flees from me once again.

Suddenly, I feel unclean. I beeline it for my bedroom closet so I can change. Calvin's skull peeks at me from behind my t-shirts, so innocent now. Like a child. I remove his skull from its hiding place and set it atop my dresser.

"How you feeling, Calvin?" I ask him, my drummer. Only now that he's digested do I feel any sort of affection for him. His hollow eye sockets and perpetual death-grin speak to me, and I find myself gazing at him from the edge of my bed, hand tucked underneath my chin as if inspecting a rare painting.

"Honestly, you look great. Better than ever. God knows your hygiene wasn't doing you any favors before, but look at you now. Glowing. What a change. I know you must be angry with me, but there's no reason we can't start fresh now. I think Lola would appreciate it."

Calvin keeps his cool and says nothing, and I have to say I very much appreciate his new complicity. If only he'd mastered this attitude a few days ago, he might still be alive.

"It occurs to me that you never got to hear my set. Perhaps I'll bring you along to my next show. You seem like the kind of guy who likes the macabre. Maybe you'll learn something about good music, for once."

The drummer smiles and smiles, and I pick him up again, cradling his fragile bones in my hands, then gently carry him into the living room, to the side table near the front door where I keep my purse.

I call out, "Lola, I'm going for a walk."

The drummer slides nicely into the cavernous bohemian sack I call my purse, and my keys make a satisfying clinking noise against the skull as I hoist the bag over my shoulder and head outside. And what a day it is! The heat prickles my skin until it becomes gooseflesh. It'll be a scorcher today, but I love the heat.

Calvin and I walk in silence. His skull can accentuate the motif of my future shows. Originally, I'd intended to play more electronica, boppy shit that a person can't help but move to, but as Disco Mama evolves, I think this is a little too pedestrian for me. I need a new angle. Honestly, I think I was too afraid to go for it before, but the drummer here is like my little rabbit's foot, my good luck charm. I feel ready now.

We traverse one block and then the next before we reach what I call Carob Tree Lane. The street name is actually Grand Sky Boulevard, but three of the ten houses have carob trees in their yards. When they're blooming, I can't smell a single thing but the mildly repulsive scent of carob. Must be one of those genetic things, because neither Jimothy or Lola can smell it, just me. When I tell them that the scent reminds me of semen, they make a face like I'd just burped into their mouths. Normally, I take great lengths to avoid this street from March through May, but today I head right for it.

The smell is a shame, really, because carob trees are rather interesting. Their fruit is used as a chocolate surrogate, which I only know because I had a cousin riddled with allergies, but that's not what interests me about them. When you live in the desert, you grow accustomed to small, bush-like trees with thorns, but carob trees grow medieval. They have thick, sturdy trunks and remind me of the gnarled prop trees used to denote evil forests on movie sets. These trees appear inhabited by mystical woodland creatures. The way their trunks split off makes them easier for height-fearing kids to climb.

Being repulsed by the blooms of these beautiful fairy trees is a betrayal I've yet to forgive. Today, however, is a day of making amends. If the drummer and I can make peace, anything is possible.

The first carob tree is three houses down and is the most majestic of them by far. The neighborhood was built in the eighties, and this tree must have been planted around that time. The tree is positioned closer to the front stoop than the street, so I must break the barrier of suburban decency to get a better look. I wander into the yard. The tree's bark is cool to the touch, the heat of afternoon unable to pierce its protective canopy. The trunk of it measures two feet at the bottom before it splits into three offshoots, two of which intertwine like lovers. Dark, emerald leaves provide a thick canopy for the ground underneath, and despite the homeowner's insistence on puke-colored gravel, small spots of moss peek through the rock near the drip line. The tree itself is a beauty, unbefitting such spartan ambiance, but then the stench of it hits me just as I think I've acclimated, and my opinion readjusts–it is exactly where it belongs.

Carob trees are sturdy things; I'd forgotten just how sturdy, and I'm a woman who appreciates strength over design. It's funny, thinking about Lola as a little girl asking me why I hate trees, and when I would tell her it wasn't all trees, just these specific trees, she'd scrunch up her little face and call me weird. To a little girl who smells nothing but open air, it must have seemed weird to hear her mother complain about the biggest trees on the block. Maybe she would hate them too if she could pick up their oily and unforgiving fragrance, or maybe she wouldn't mind it.

Perhaps that's been the problem all along–where others find nothing, I invent distaste.

The moment of this revelation is precisely when the owner of the house cracks open their front door and asks me what I'm doing in their yard.

"Just admiring your tree."

She's older than me, but not by much, and wears frustration on her face like an overnight mask. "I hate that tree," she says.

"Then why do you keep it?"

She scowls. Give her a cast iron pan and she, too, might have hurled it.

"Get off my property."

"You know," I say. "These trees smell like shit."

"Do I need to call the cops?"

"Do whatever suits you, honey," I say. Before leaving, I yank one of the bean pods from the branch directly over my head. I drop it into the drummer's eye socket just inside my purse. I nod before turning on my heel to leave.

Every fold of my body is slick with sweat by the end of my stroll, so much so that Lola makes a sour face when I return. She's sitting on the bottom step of our stairs, elbows perched on her knees and leaning her right cheek on a balled fist.

"What's wrong?"

"Emily wants to come over."

"Today? Why?"

I don't know, but she sounded weird. Upset."

"What on earth does that little brat have to be sad about?"

"Mom–"

I wave away her rant before it gains traction. "It's fine. Guess we're getting Thai food again tonight."

Lola nods, her phone appearing in her palm like a magic trick. "I'll ask her what she wants. Also, Dad finally called. He wants you to call him back."

"He cracked quicker than I thought," I say.

"Grandma just died; why can't you give him a break?"

"Because I am a huge bitch, Lola. He knew that when he married me. Too late to complain about it now."

However, as the words leave my lips, I am not so sure this is true. I was a bitch from the start, but I suspect that Jimothy has always considered my attitude some kind of puzzling layer only he had the capacity to crack. Back in our club days, we both got off from the cat and mouse pursuit. He chased, I ran, and then we fucked vigorously when we collided. Just when Jimothy threatened to break into my inner sanctum, I fled for good. The second time we connected, I had a buffer named Lola to keep him far enough away. Anything to prevent this man willing to love me from seeing the tar pit where my heart should be.

The look on my daughter's face levels me right then and there. I can read every thought going through her head, as clearly as Disco Mama's scrolling marquee. She truly hates me. She might not know yet that she hates me, but one day she will recount this conversation to a therapist who will call me a narcissist while passing the tissues to my poor, downtrodden adult child. Then they'll try to treat her, try to ease her suffering and PTSD. They'll plod through her traumatic childhood for years before they realize how outgunned they really are, because Lola is me. As much as Jimothy tries–hell, however much *I* might try–she is me, to her very core. And that's a cough no syrup can cure.

No time is wasted before I am dialing my dear husband. My call goes directly to voicemail, but before I can leave a message a text message notification vibrates against my ear.

I've booked a flight home for next week. Tying up loose ends here before you and I have a talk

A talk? Does this mean I can't go to prom?

If I wanted to discuss this now I would have answered your call

Can't wait, honey

Don't start with that shit. You quit your job without telling me!

I got another one, but you never asked about that. Regardless, happy flight. See you soon

I chuck my phone into the plush comforter of my bed and hold my breath as I await the notification of Jimothy's response, but it doesn't come. This might finally be the fight that cracks the dam. He's probably researching divorce attorneys as we speak. The idea of him sitting in his hotel diligently planning the implosion of his life at home bugs the shit out me, almost like he beat me to the punch. Sadness floats like a loose hair in front of my eyes, but it's easy to dismiss. I never thought our marriage would last as long as it has, and the reason for that very well could be because we have never spent this much time apart. Maybe he intrinsically knew I would spiral into a different being in his absence, so he dared not leave. We got comfortable, I guess, distracted by parenthood and mortgage payments and the basic tedium of American existence. I wonder if we ever loved each other. In the beginning, we couldn't peel away from one another, always sucking on each other like two lampreys. Good sex, drugs, and volcanic hormones can mimic love so seamlessly we would never know the difference. Maybe that's all love is anyway. No shame in admitting it, no shame in letting it die a natural death.

I flick away my emotions and text Cris.

You got a date for the next show yet?

He says a month unless someone backs out

You have the lineup?

No, but I'll get it

Great. Let's destroy that stage, Cris.

❂ ❂ ❂

Emily arrives (late) at the house, after six in the evening. Our dinner time is early by typical standards, so while Lola waited for her friend to eat, I did not. The girls were microwaving their food while mine already rolled around distastefully in my stomach. Too soon to eat again, I suppose.

I try not to be too obvious in my eavesdropping, but give up all pretenses after Emily says, "Not even his roommate knows where he is."

"Knows where who is?" I ask.

Emily's gaze darts to Lola, who rolls her eyes and says, "She knows, Emily."

"I didn't know you told her."

"She told me everything," I say. The shock on Emily's face is genuine, but the guilt that comes pouring out after is entirely manufactured–eyes big and wide, hand over heart. Poor thing has no idea how obvious she is. What teenager does?

Emily says, "I told her she shouldn't lie to you."

Sure you did, hon.

Lola holds up her hand just out of Emily's line of sight. She's begging me to let it go.

Fat chance. I ask, "That's neither here nor there. Is that who you were talking about just now? The drummer boy?"

Emily nods. "Yeah, he's missing or something. No one knows where he is."

"Did you check the high school? He seems to have a lot of business there," I say.

It takes Lola's crestfallen expression to remind me that she still likes this guy and is worried about him. I'll never reconcile what he was with what she saw in him, but my disdain changes nothing in her eyes. Probably makes him more desirable, even though he was such an asshole to her.

"Anyway," I say. "Lola did break up with him, and considering the age difference I can understand lying low a while. Maybe he thinks I'll call the cops on him."

"Mom!" Lola snaps.

The suggestion settles nicely with Emily, though. "That would make a lot of sense, actually."

"Take it from me, girls. Guys like him are always a flight risk. If you ask me, he's done you both a tremendous favor."

Satisfied, Emily retrieves her dinner from the microwave and nearly skips to the table, leaving Lola and I in a split-second standoff. An outsider might not catch it, but that girl was sizing me up, predator versus predator, looking for a crack in my façade. Another moment longer and I might have smiled, and right then she'd have known I was involved in his disappearance, but Emily called her attention away by asking for a glass of water.

The rest of dinner passes in usual form: phone passing, giggles, dread over their upcoming chemistry exam. I leave them to it, occasionally passing by with a laundry basket full of clothes I never intend to put away or emptying the dishwasher. They pay me little attention, and by the looks of it act as if the past few weeks never happened. They're back on track. While I feel relief for my daughter's feelings and social standing, there is also my disappointment in her choice of friend. This break-up-and-make-up cycle will only repeat itself in another few months. It always does with Emily.

Just as I'm beginning to get bored, Cris texts me with the CLA$$H lineup for the next few weeks. Naturally, I don't recognize any of the other acts, nor do I care about them, aside from one–a DJ calling himself Jesus Hands.

I don't know anything about him either, just that he is performing this upcoming Friday and I want that slot.

Who the fuck is jesus hands. Is he for real?

He's from California, I guess. The new wonderkid. Marcus is obsessed

We need his slot

He's been locked in for months. It'll never happen

If you want another show, it's Friday or nothing

The rat house might take us

Fuck the rat house. It's beneath us

You know you JUST played there

So what

How does your husband not know about all this?

Don't worry about that. Find a club. I've got a setlist brewing

My rate increased btw

I'll pay you whatever you want if you make this happen. Name your price.

I don't care about the money, as long as she helps me succeed. I wait. No response. We both know I've won. I send a final message.

Get to work, then

Chapter 17

My next few hours are consumed with learning every-thing I can about Jesus Hands. He's young: I could be his mother. Every official picture on his social media shows him backlit by neon lights with a moody expression on his face. He's really forcing the tortured genius angle. His barely-legal fans seem to eat it up.

Texting Marcus for more information is easier than I anticipated. He is all too eager to explain to me how he managed to score an act like "JH," as he describes him. He shares everything, down to the name of Jesus Hands's agent, the city where he lives, the day and time he arrives, and where JH will be staying. Part of me feels guilty for putting a tool like Marcus in the middle of my scheming–I will get that spot on Friday–but the sentiment fades the instant he mistakenly sends me a text meant for someone else.

This old bitch is delusional if she thinks I'm bumping JH

I don't respond to this. He doesn't either. Whether or not it was intentional, neither of us address it again. He might not even care about offending me, which is fine. Why should he? His insolence gives me a great idea, though. Maybe I'll send him a thank-you card after I perform in a slot meant for JH.

Emily stays the night, or I assume she does because I never hear her leave. The girls are suspiciously quiet upstairs. I pause my internet sleuthing every once and a while to spy on them, and to see if I can grab any bits of their gossip. But these two are professionals, and I can't gather anything of use. At some point, I fall asleep at my computer only to jerk away as someone slams a cabinet door in the kitchen. It's morning and the girls are looking for cereal.

Emily sits at the table as Lola fetches two bowls and a giant bag of apple rings. My instinct is to ask Emily how her legs are healing, considering it's too much for her to walk and get her own bowl, but the comment isn't worth the price of Lola's embarrassed fury. Instead, I sit quietly across from my daughter's friend while Lola grabs some clean spoons from the dishwasher. I stare right at Emily. Even though the girl deftly avoids my eye contact, my gaze alone is uncomfortable enough to make her peel her ass from the chair and help, if only to get away from me.

In this moment, I observe my daughter with her friend, truly observe her—how she awkwardly smiles when they bump into each other, her easy little laugh masking a muted terror behind her eyes. Her movements are slightly robotic, as if she doesn't know how to behave. She's in love with Emily, I realize, perhaps not in a sexual way, but a desperate way. Lola would like nothing more than for Emily's complete attention, her affection, her acceptance. But Emily is a shark, a thing with teeth that never stops chewing. Even if Lola entertains her, to Emily she is nothing but meat. This reminds me of Calvin, whose remains are tucked ever-so-nicely in my purse. He thought the same thing about Lola, saw her as an appetizer before a big meal, and I wonder why she welcomes so many predators to circle her when she's so vicious at home. Some of it is just being an ungainly teenager, some of it is because she's aesthetically beautiful, and some of it is because she doesn't know any better–the most terrifying predator in her life is her own mother.

In this regard, I have inhibited her awareness. Where I think I've sharpened her teeth, I've ground her ego to a nub instead. Perhaps the drummer wasn't the problem after all, but a symptom.

"Girls," I say. Both of them freeze and glare at me, as if I'd spit in their food. "Tonight, I think we should go out."

✿ ✿ ✿

It took an entire day of cajoling to get both teenagers on board with my impromptu field trip, but like a good mother, I ply them with vodka to get them warmed up to the idea. Lola is ready to fight me, her eyes narrowing at me with fierce distaste, until Emily squeals with delight.

"Your mom is fucking awesome," she says as she slams back-to-back shots like an old pro. No coughing, no chaser. Where are this girl's parents?

"Where are we going?" Emily asks.

Lola holds her little shot of liquor carefully and I can sense her hackles raise, I grab my purse and my keys wait by the door.

"I thought we'd check out the Rat House tonight."

"Cool," Emily says. "Maybe you-know-who is playing and we can finally find out where he's been."

But Lola isn't looking at Emily. She's locked eyes with me instead.

"Why do you want to go there?" she asks me.

"I made friends with the bartender the night I followed you," I say.

Lola shrugs, her shock either faded or masked so articulately one would never know she was bothered at all. Makes me wonder just how high she was that night. How far would things have progressed with Calvin had I not been there to stop it?

"I assume your dad won't mind?" I ask Emily.

"He doesn't give a shit."

I'd have to agree, considering it's a Sunday night and I've not heard a word from either of her parents, wondering where she is.

The Rat House is packed so I have to park on the next street over. I grumble, "What the fuck is going on here?"

Emily pulls Lola by the wrist to the front door without me. Smoothly, the girls display their fake IDs. The doorman appears to recognize them and waves them through with hardly a glance. They disappear inside before I even reach the door.

"You know they're underage," I say as I reach the entry. "Tsk, tsk."

He responds with a blasé *whatever* before taking an extra moment to look at my face. "Hey, you're Disco Mama, aren't you? Hank will want to see you."

"Oh, good. Maybe I can convince him to fire you for letting children into the bar."

The innards of the Rat House are just as packed as its parking lot. I spy the girls huddled in a corner near the stage, leaning into each other to speak over the churn of people. There isn't a single empty seat at the bar, but I squeeze my way to the front of the line with little effort. People don't complain when you move with purpose. They just assume you work there.

Hank spots me as I erupt through the commotion like Moses parting the Red Sea.

"Hello, Hank," I say. "How's business?"

He looks me up and down before pouring me a drink on the house. At least, I assume it's on the house. "I need to talk to you."

"You want me back? Is that it?"

"Absolutely not."

He returns to his customers, pouring drinks like a machine. Resting my elbows on the bar, I scan the crowd for anyone I know. Part of me expects the drummer to waltz onto the stage, eyes locked onto Lola, but that's impossible, his head being stuffed into my purse and all. Maybe I'll leave his skull at the Rat House, in memoriam. Maybe I'll run it over with my car. I haven't decided.

A familiar sensation tugs at all the little hairs on my body, and I shudder at the eerie feeling of being watched. I glance around and spot no one; nobody is making eye contact or lingering a beat too long in my direction. Maybe it's the drummer, his ghost screaming for someone to see me and save him from his captor. The girls are still merrily ignoring my presence. Nobody sees me, but the sensation refuses to fade.

Having hit a lull in orders, Hank nods toward the stage, indicating to meet him in the back. I wave at the girls as I follow him. Neither wave back.

Hank wastes no time laying into me. "I don't know what you did, and I'm not going to say shit, but the cops came around the other night. What exactly did you do to that dumbass going after your daughter?"

"I told him I'd call the cops if he ever came near her again. Why?"

Hank rolls his shoulders, back straight as a rod. "You know, it's funny. You wander in here one night and all hell breaks loose after. The boy is missing."

"So what? He's a loser."

"I've heard some batshit stories in my life, but nothing quite as ludicrous as the ones involving you, Disco Mama. You know that's why they're all here."

"Who? The cops?"

"No," he points toward the bar. "All those customers."

My urge to speak is briefly quieted by bewilderment. "None of them wanted to see me when I was performing. Why now?"

"Rumors spread quickly," he says. "Somehow Disco Mama and the missing man have been mashed together into one glob of intrigue."

"How is that possible?"

"Whatever you think of them, Beefy Reefer is a staple at the Rat House. They have a small, local following. Their drummer going missing has become somewhat of a scandal."

"How does that involve me?"

Hank shrugs. "He had a lot to say about you before he disappeared. I think some of these people think you are some kind of demon. Good or bad, they want to catch a glimpse of you."

From the corner of the bar near the front door I catch sight of the doorman pointing towards the stage. "Hank, did you happen to tell your doorman about the drummer's tall tale?"

"No," he says. "But he was working that night when it all went down. I can only assume he overheard what happened. Don't come back to my bar or I'll have no choice but to tell the cops. They're looking for you." He brushes past me to return to his post.

Stopping his retreat by the sleeve of his shirt, I ask him why he didn't give me up already.

"I'm not stupid, that's why." Before thoroughly escaping me, he advises me to use the back door to leave. More people are pointing my way, and a buzz vibrates the small bar so that it feels like the drywall might slough away from the pressure of it. Adrenaline jolts my body into action, and before the girls can catch wind of what's happening, I've got them both by the collars and am all but dragging them through the back. These people think I've killed him. They know I've killed him.

Lola yells at me and demands to know what I'm doing, why we're leaving when we just arrived, what did that bartender guy say to me, *what's wrong, what's wrong!* But I don't answer. Nothing is wrong, sweetie. Nothing is wrong. I've got Calvin's skull clutched against my chest as we speed to the car, and only once the doors are closed and locked do I speak.

"Mom! What happened?"

"That shithead says I owe him money," I say.

Lola freezes, immediately catching the lie that Emily does not.

"For what?" Emily asks.

"I bought some weed from him. He's trying to hustle me."

Lola is silent. She knows I'm lying. Emily, on the other hand, appears completely unfazed by my admission.

"What an asshole," Emily says. "It should be legal by now, anyway."

"Consider this a life lesson. When a dealer gets you cornered and demands cash you don't have, bug the fuck out as fast as possible."

On the way home, Lola stares daggers at me every time our eyes meet in the rearview mirror. Emily obliviously yammers on about the injustice of criminalizing a plant. By the time we return to the house, she's midway through her harrowing tale of puking after an amateurishly huge bong rip. She asks for more vodka before the front door even has time to close behind us.

"Knock yourself out," I say. "But only one." The last thing I want to deal with right now is someone else's teenager getting alcohol poisoning.

Emily pours herself a shot, downs it easily, then leaves to use the bathroom down the hall. Arms crossed, face sour as a lemon, Lola leans into me the second her friend is out of earshot.

"You're lying."

"Yeah? How would you know?"

"You'd never buy weed. Plus, that bartender doesn't look like he deals. I don't think you even smoke weed."

"What are you getting at, Lola?"

She bites back her words with her teeth, drawing blood from her bottom lip. "I'm going upstairs."

"If Emily barfs on the bed, I'm not cleaning it up," I shout after her, but she slams her bedroom door mid-sentence.

I grab the vodka by the neck of the bottle and let the clear poison burn away my nerves.

Chapter 18

I spend the night dreaming and making plans. The next day, Emily sleeps until noon; Lola appears long enough to wave her friend goodbye. As soon as our little guest is gone and Lola sealed into her bedroom, I send Cris a flurry of texts.

At first, Cris is baffled by my wild ideas but soon catches my drift after I describe the hubbub at the Rat House.

Ride the wave of intrigue before it dies on the sand, Cris. That's how stars are made.

We are going to get that Jesus Hands time slot. I'm certain of it. Disco Mama has a fleeting wisp of street cred now. I just have to let the rumor mill know where I'll be—and soon, before my ubiquity dissolves.

I spend most of the day curating a set; that will give Cris as much time as possible to prepare the rest of the show. I tell Cris to be fucking ready, because we are playing whether Marcus likes it or not. Marcus is still staunchly keeping Jesus Hands in the slot I want, but I've got a plan and Cris is on board. She's worked enough with me to trust me–as far as she knows I haven't steered her wrong yet. I pull a thousand dollars out of my savings account on my way home. If anyone will put this money to good use, it's Cris. She's earned it. Then I go to the print shop to make flyers.

By this point, neither Lola nor Jimothy are speaking to me, which is just as well, since most of my time is dedicated to preparing for the show. This will be the show, I can feel it. There's a finality about it, settling like a stone in my gut every time I think about it. This only means it is that much more important that I don't fuck it up.

Monday, I send emails to JH and his agent.

Tuesday, I litter the streets with blood-red flyers.

Wednesday, I receive a text from Cris.

You'll never guess what happened. JH backed out

I'll admit I was beginning to worry that he wouldn't, and seeing this confirmation untwisted the knot squeezing my ribcage. My plan is working.

Thursday, I return to the Rat House, where I tape, staple, and toss more flyers on every open spot available. This eats up about half of my remaining inventory. I spread the rest onto every lamppost, mailbox, and windshield within a one-mile radius of Marcus' club.

DISCO MAMA
FINAL PERFORMANCE
I'LL TELL YOU EVERYTHING
FRIDAY NIGHT, CLA$$H, 9PM

Cris continues to text me throughout the night, having received multiple angry phone calls from Marcus.

He says he'll never let you play there again. Says he'll call the cops if you show up

Like fuck he will. Believe me, he'll let us in when he sees how many people I bring with me.

With flyers?

With reputation. The Rat House crew thinks I killed someone. My flyers promise to reveal the truth if they come to our show. Wouldn't you want to go to a show like that?

Did you really kill someone?

I guess you'll have to come to find out ;)

I'm not even thinking of Jimothy, who is scheduled to arrive home Monday morning. Poor fool has no idea what he's coming home to–or maybe he does.

Once, many years ago and after copious amounts of tequila shots, I asked Jimothy what he ever saw in me to begin with. Despite all his wicked charm and sharp wits, he and I were never a pair. Neither of our families saw our relationship coming. I used to think Jimothy was a wrangler and I a beast; that he loved having something wild to manage because it made him feel strong and important and capable. To be fair, this very well could have been part of the initial attraction, but as we age and grow apart, as I see the small ways he inserts himself between me and Lola, how he protects her, buffers her, loves her, throws himself to me as a shield, as his mother dies and he comforts her through his veil of loathing for her very being, I understand the truth of it–he hates Marilyn, and he hates me too, always has, and that's all he knows how to do.

How sad for him. I didn't force him to marry a narcissist like his mother. He could have been anything. I see that now. He could have been the hero he always dreamed of. Instead, he wasted his warmth and light trying to keep me from slipping into a bog of my own creation, and now that I'm here, now that I've made it, there is no way in hell I'm ever coming out of my muck again.

By Thursday evening, I have slipped into a brand-new type of delirium. I do not eat, only drink coffee and chew an occasional piece of gum. For most of the afternoon, I don't know where Lola is. I have no idea if she is even home or if she's run away with Emily or already camping out at the airport, waiting for her dad to come home. Certainly, she misses him. I'm sure I'd miss my dad too, if I'd had one.

Every time my eyes close I see a stage; I see people and their black-orb eyes gazing lovingly at me. I feel the music in my chest, the bass disrupting my heartbeat like a strike of lightning. I feel powerful, even adored. All I ever wanted was to be adored. What girl doesn't?

A slamming door shocks me out of my head. The house is shadowy and dark as night takes up residence. Lola is returning home from wherever she's been. I don't even know if she's been to school. All the lights are out because I haven't needed them to sit aimlessly and think.

"Mom?" she calls, and when I don't respond she sighs (with relief? Who knows.) and begins speaking to someone on the phone.

"She's not home," she says. "Yeah. I know. I'm going to grab some clothes and head to Emily's. Yeah. I love you, too."

I wonder how much she's told her father? I can only assume everything, all our dirty little secrets; the club, the vodka, my irrational hours. It's evident I have lost every ounce of her loyalty, and so now there is little reason to maintain idiotic pretenses.

I'm cross-legged on my unmade bed, the drummer's skull in my lap, listening to my child stomp around hurriedly in her room as she packs to leave me once and for all. I knew this day would come–it always comes–but I'm far calmer than I envisioned. Maybe that's because I know she's not going anywhere. At least not tonight.

My bones pop as I untangle myself from the quilt. With the drummer tucked under my arm, I slink to the bottom of the staircase and wait. The lights are on in the bathroom as Lola rips through drawers. The medicine cabinet opens and slams shut. She sloppily slaps each item into her bag with a carelessness which points to her panic. That eyeshadow palette was a limited edition, but she handles it like it was a bottlecap. I can feel the way her pulse pounds in her throat. I can almost see it.

She doesn't bother flipping off the light as she exits the bathroom. All I see as she squares up at the top of the stairs is her dark silhouette haloed by offensive fluorescent beams.

She drops her bags when she spots me but doesn't yelp. I've finally managed to scare the argument out of her.

"You're home," she says.

"I never left."

She doesn't take her eyes off me even as she kneels to retrieve her bag. "I'm going to Emily's house."

"Are you?"

"Is that okay?" There's a hitch in her voice.

"Since when do you care what I think?"

Lola's mood is thick with uncertainty. "I'll call you when I get there to let you know I'm safe."

Safe. What a choice of words.

"I want to show you something." I float towards the darkened kitchen, setting the skull centerpiece on the table. Lola begrudgingly follows, maintaining a steady five paces between us. I take my usual seat at the end of the table and motion for Lola to take hers.

"Why are the lights off?" she asks.

"Turn them on, if you like."

The dining room chandelier flicks alive. Lola gasps with surprise at the sight of the skull. "Mom, what is that?"

"Your boyfriend."

Her face scrunches. She doesn't believe me. "That's not funny."

"I won't be here by the time your dad returns."

"You're moving?"

I nod once. "Probably. I don't think this marriage is tenable anymore."

"Was it ever?"

Drumming my fingers against the table, I lean in closer. "I wonder if you say such things to him, or only to me?"

"I'm a lot like Dad. We talk."

"I know I've never been the kind of mom you needed, but you are nothing like your dad."

Lola crosses her arms as if trying to keep herself upright. "What does *that* mean?"

I feel cold all over. Empty. Lying no longer serves me.

"I want to offer something to you that I'll never offer again. I suggest you consider what I am about to say carefully, because I have never given it to anyone before nor will I ever again. Not even to your father."

"What is it?"

The back of the chair creaks as I lean into it. "The truth."

"How could I ever believe that you're telling the truth?"

"My patience is limited."

She rises. "You know what? I don't care, Mom. I don't care about anything you have to say."

My voice is volcanic. "Sit down!"

I am done playing games. Done pretending. Done allowing Jimothy the Usurper to manipulate *my* daughter. It's time for her to see who I really am. Otherwise, she'll never understand herself and let insolent, sappy men run roughshod over her. Time to shed her skin, embrace the viper that she is. Just like her mother.

"Ask me something," I say.

She hesitates. She doesn't want to play my game, but I've frightened her into submission. "Are you really a DJ?"

"This is your burning question? Yes, I am. My next show is tomorrow."

Her eyes flick toward the skull and back to me. Her real question is evident, but she's afraid to ask it.

"Have you ever loved Dad?"

"Yes, probably. It's hard to say what love is, but I think I did love him."

"Did?" She's quiet for a few moments, head down and picking at her cuticles. We both keep our words tucked tight to our chests like bombs on a countdown. The wrong question might set us off. Lola feels it, I know she does, and she's afraid. She should be. Fear teaches you things you'll never learn otherwise.

She points to the skull. "That's not Dad, is it?" She smiles, trying to lighten the mood. Maybe distract me.

"No. And it's not Jimmy's, either."

Her head jerks up. She doesn't say a word, but I see the pain of that truth land. Jimothy and I agreed to never discuss her parentage. As far as she was concerned, he was her father. We even had her birth certificate amended. We figured it was better for her development, but now I know what a mistake that was. She's always assumed she was above her true station, when in reality she's the product of a faceless one-night stand with a man who likely puked himself to death in an alley before she turned one.

Denying her the truth has made her soft. Lola can't afford to be soft. It's clear I can't protect her anymore. It's time for her to protect herself.

She's crying, and I am torn between comforting her and maintaining my composure.

"You're lying," she says.

"I'm not, and you know I'm not. Part of you had to have known."

She stares me down, not bothering to wipe away her tears. "Why are you saying all this to me now?"

I lean forward. "I know your greatest fear is turning into me. It was my greatest fear, too. Turns out avoidance and denial doesn't fix the problem, because I'm not only *like* my mother; I am infinitely worse. You'll never evolve without understanding where you came from."

"Fuck you." She speaks the curse like a proclamation read from parchment.

I'm proud. Her fury gives me hope. "Tell me, Lola, what on earth did you ever see in that drummer?"

She looks at me as if I'm a buffoon. "Why do you care, Mom? Why do you care so much about him? He liked me. That's really all it was, but you went apeshit, acting like I was going to marry the guy. I know he was fucking stupid, but he liked me."

"Of course he was stupid, but that doesn't mean he wasn't dangerous. Men like that are very good at ruining people's lives."

"And that means, what? You wanted to ruin me yourself?"

Her sudden ferocity makes me laugh, which only spurs her to her feet to leave. She freezes as I catch her by the arm.

"I'm going to Emily's," she says.

I nod toward the skull. "It's his, you know."

"What do you mean?"

I shove her back into her chair a little more forcefully than I intended, but she gets the message and sits, every muscle visible in her neck and arms pulled like taut rope.

"Calvin came to the house one night with a backpack full of spray paint. I thought he was an intruder, and I suppose he was. Caught him just as he was about to write something on the garage door."

Again, I lean in for emphasis. My fingers are jittery from my sudden spike of adrenaline as I recall that night. "Do you see what I mean, Lola? He was dumb and dangerous. With all his shit-talking, what do you think he was going to write on our garage? 'Lola, you beautiful perfect woman, please come back to me? I love you?' No, more like 'slut' or 'whore' or 'bitch.' And we could have it repainted by noon the next day, but that's all anyone would ever remember about you. 'Whore.' People remember emotion better than anything. Heartbreak resonates. They might commiserate with you, feel for you, but they'll still refer to you as a whore. That's just how it is."

I'm angry now. Furious. I wish I'd had someone sit me down and explain these things when I was young. This is the kind of shit my mom should have done for me. If she'd murdered one of my shitty high school boyfriends I'd at least have known she loved me, in her own, deranged way.

Lola does not scream, doesn't cry anymore, just glares at the skull in disbelief. I think she's afraid that a sudden noise might spook me. "Are you telling me that you killed him?"

"Smashed his head in with a cast iron skillet. See?" The skull fracture reads easily in the overhead light. I point to the crack, my index finger the meteor sailing towards the crater in his bone.

Lola's face looks sickly but still, she does not move. "If that's really Calvin, where is the rest of him?"

"Why, you going to rescue his remains?"

"Why do you have his skull, Mom? How is it so clean? Where is the rest of him?"

I wave her questions away. "Let the cops look for him. I'm sure that's the first place you'll go once you're free."

Her façade is cracking now. Here come the tears. "Are you really a murderer?"

The pitch of her voice strikes my senses like an ice pick, the throb of irritation ringing on a loop. She starts to cry again.

"He was such a loser, Lola. I can't fathom why *you* care. Although I will say, he's a lot more pleasant now that he's dead." I can sense the pressure of her body, the way it threatens to snap open as if on a spring, to flee, to run, to save herself. "Baby," I say, voice low, as if cooing to a newborn. "Do you know what mother animals do in the wild to protect their young? They fight like hell. They fight with their teeth. They kill and maim. Motherhood is ferocious and disgusting. It is animalistic. *We* are animals."

Her face mutates, but I cut her off before she can ask the question I already read on her lips. She is going to ruin my plans, and she's the only one who knows how. The second I let her go, she will call the cops and ensure I never make it to my show.

"You know what mothers do when their babies get in the way? I'll tell you what they do. They swallow those babies whole."

Lola leaps to her feet, but not quick enough. I catch her by the throat as she tries to scramble away from me. A whack to her windpipe stops her cold and she crumples to the floor, grasping her throat and sucking wildly for air.

"The babies who survive their mother will survive anything. All fear is gone, stripped away by the gullet of their creator. I've failed you child, desperately failed you. Now you'll learn to fear and to fight, or you'll die. But I don't think you'll stop living, Lola. You are such a little bitch that I think you'll kill me from the inside out."

She's gulping for a breath that never comes. Injury and her panic steal every opportunity of oxygen, and without air, she doesn't fuss all that much. Not at first. My lower jaw pops free with one, vicious punch, and I can only imagine the terror she feels as I drool over her, my slack-hanging jaw unable to contain my fluids. Within seconds, she faints. It makes the start of this so much easier.

Eating Lola is more delightful than I ever could have imagined. I lean in to inhale her, my mouth sagging to the floor, skin like putty, every muscle responding just as it was meant to—orifices just open up on women, that's what they do. Our bodies are brutal but they respect a knowing mistress, so to slide the citrusy head of my child inside my mouth and into my gasping throat is easy. Painful, yes, but easy because the body does its work. This is not like Calvin, who all but squished into an easy paste–Lola is firm. Supple. She is alive, and soon she is thrashing for her life.

Everything begins with the head. Even snakes swallow their meals headfirst, and by the time Lola regains enough consciousness to fight me, I've already got her shoulders by my teeth. She knocks a few of my teeth out, sure, but she's strangled by my gullet. Her struggling makes my job more frustrating, but not impossible. I can't breathe anymore, but I don't need to breathe. It's like when my music plays. I'm somewhere else, in a dream, the room is dark and the drummer watches with malice filling the hollow spaces of his skull. I feel those empty sockets like hot pokers, and I feel my daughter kicking me, kicking me all over again, and there is no pain, no discomfort, I just am. I do. I perform. There are stars in my vision, firework pockets of lights radiating my retinas, burning them. My cells are screaming in distress but I don't feel it.

My ribs spring open to make room for Lola as I swallow her down, like a snake does a rat. I swell and stretch, organs displacing into the hidden void of my insides where my humanity should have been. I feel every bit of my daughter ripping me apart on the way down, the top of her head gutting my insides to make room for the rest of her.

When I'm down to her knees, the skin of my neck breaks apart, held only by the flimsiest strands of middle-aged collagen. I rip apart into ridges and scales as I absorb my near-grown daughter inside me. She fights–oh, does she fight, especially as I tear off her shoes, breaking glass as I hurl them off her feet before they go down with the rest of her. I don't like sneakers. Not one little bit.

My clothes are tight, my shirt rising over the bulge in my belly and bunching around my breasts. Luckily, I'm wearing sweats or else I might have torn my jeans. Still, Lola fights. I feel her inside me wriggling like a worm. Every shift elicits a current of delicious pain that rings like a gong amongst my bones, and I love it, it's a good pain, the aftershock pain of hard work. Spitting one of my upper canines into my palm–she kicked it out on her way in–I get her all the way down. She is squirming and she's pissed, but she is down. She is contained.

If she wants to free herself or be digested, the decision is now up to her.

I lay on the floor for what seems like hours, daydreaming mostly. For a while, Lola rages intensely inside me, but after a while she simmers, only disturbing my solace to hiccup, or perhaps sob. I imagine her inside me again, gooey with fluid, trapped and gasping, calm. I feel her sleeping, for what else is there for her to do? The drummer's skull watches me from the top of the table. More than once, my body goes suddenly cold, like a window thrown open on a snowy night, like my body is hollowed out by a gust of ice, because I see Lola next to him–her slightly smaller skull next to his, and I seem to hear their skulls clacking like baby rattles inside the pouch of my purse as we stroll around on walks, and the thought is so chilling a wave of nausea sweeps over me, threatening to pour her right out again onto the kitchen floor. But I'm versed enough in emotional avoidance to leave those dark thoughts behind, ignore them, forget about them. I exorcise them from my psyche completely, eventually dozing from exhaustion. Next to me, Lola's phone lights up like fireworks with texts and missed calls I don't bother to check. Somewhere else in my dark, cavernous home my own phone buzzes endlessly, too. I'll answer it to see my show come to fruition. Then, I'm awakened by knocking on the front door.

Dread grips my chest. It might be Jimothy, home early, but no. Jimothy wouldn't knock.

I must take care to stand myself upright as the sudden bulge of my belly throws off my equilibrium, but after a few sluggish steps I'm back to my usual stride. A third knock comes accompanied by the small, worried squeak of a young girl on the other side of the door.

"Lola?"

Emily. Lola was planning to sleep over. As if hearing her friend's voice, Lola twists inside of me. Her elbow pokes at my torso and the sensation of her struggling to open her arms feels like the jaws of life tugging at my pelvis. My baby is going to make me suffer, that little bitch.

I open the door enough to poke my head through.

She squeaks, "Is Lola here? She was going to come over, but she never showed up and now she's not answering my calls."

"She decided to stay home after all. She's fine."

"Can I talk to her?"

"No."

"No?"

"That's what I said. She's grounded. I took her phone."

Emily stares at the chipping paint of the front door, afraid to make eye contact but also hesitant to leave. "She's been sending some weird messages."

"She's not doing well at the moment. I think it's the whole boyfriend thing, or maybe the fact that her best friend was spreading horseshit lies about her all over school. I don't know, what do you think is the problem?"

"I didn't–"

Popping the door open another few inches, I lean toward Emily and hiss, just enough to make her step back. "Don't lie to me, little one. You're out of your depth."

She quiets, summoning every reserve of strength in her entire soul to muster her next sentence. "She thinks you killed her boyfriend." Sweat beads on her hairline. She still can't make eye contact.

Lola, Lola, Lola. I'd call her clever if she hadn't gone and spoiled the compliment by talking to this nitwit. I laugh in Emily's face. Lola reacts to my gyrations by kicking at my throat, which winds me immediately. Emily leans over me as I hunch with my hands on my knees.

"Are you okay?" she asks.

"Yeah," I say. "I'm fine." I welcome Emily into the house with a gesture. She steps inside, jumping at the click of the deadbolt behind her.

"Now," I say, placing a guiding hand on Emily's shoulder. "Let me take you to Lola."

Chapter 19

Marcus blocks my entrance to CLA$$H. He refuses to let me inside the building, claiming I was the perpetrator behind the "evil and malicious emails" Jesus Hands had received, messages that drove him to back out of his contract. A line of people wrapped around the building, beginning four hours before the club even opens. Marcus wrongfully assumed they were there for Jesus Hands, which contributed to his seething and immediate hatred of the sight of me as he imagined the public stoning he was to receive when he informed them the show was canceled. I can tell Marcus wants to physically push me away from his club, but my swollen figure repulses him enough to stay his hands.

"I'll call the cops," he threatens.

"Talk to *them*," I say, pointing to the crowd. "If they tell you they're here for Jesus Hands and not me, I'll leave right now."

"You're insane. I saw your fucking flyers."

"I know, but they worked. Go ask."

"I'm not your employee," he says.

"I know why you wanted Jesus Hands for tonight. You're just like Cris. You want prestige. Notoriety. We all do. I'm telling you, if you let me perform tonight, you'll become a legend."

"I'll be a joke."

"Ask your customers, Marcus. Then, I promise I'll leave. Or we can wait for the cops and make an even bigger scene."

This is the threat that lands, because he believes it. He positions himself in front of the door, addressing the growing line with a cracking voice. "What show are you here to see?" he screams.

The response is a resounding wail of my stage name. They are here for Disco Mama.

While this turn of events forces Marcus to let me inside, it does not preclude him from staring at my swollen belly from behind the bar as he pours himself shot after shot of Patròn Silver. I claim my place in the middle of the stage, legs crossed, rubbing the taut skin of my torso and grimacing under the pain of Lola's dissent. By now the drummer's body was all but mush, but Lola is unrelenting in her pursuit of freedom. My midsection undulates in a visceral wave.

Cris flits around me like a little gnat, asking questions I don't care to answer, and I ignore her until she finally gives up trying to speak to me. She, too, can't stop staring at my belly, and though I'm not entirely mentally present, I do catch her whispering, "You better not die before the show."

A glass bottle clinks against the bar, now empty in Marcus's hands.

"Pour me one too, if you're going to be obnoxious about it," I say. His attitude is really fucking up my little preshow moment of zen. A drink might be what I need to fall back into it.

"Aren't you pregnant or something?" he asks.

"My wallet's in my bag–grab my Visa and charge whatever the fuck you want, but bring me my drink first."

Marcus pours, not bothering with my purse. "If you want it, come and get it," he says before walking away into the shadows of the club. Insolent little shit can't even deliver a proper drink to a lady.

Only briefly, it is quiet. The rustling of employees arriving for work, the scooting of chairs into place, the buzz of the vacuum cleaner–all of it ceases and I'm alone, aside from the people I brought with me. Pain centers me in a way nothing else can. It distracts my restless brain, forcing all attention to it. I have no choice. Pain always demands attention. Lola must know this, since we are entwined and she can feel the way my muscles tense with her every shift, twirl, and jab. She makes use of our connection often.

Doctor's claim that fetuses can hear their mothers' voices from inside the womb, and I assume this situation is no different. I tell her, "Fuck up my show and I'll shit you out on stage, child."

Lola responds with a sharp stab to my insides that stings like a hot needle. The bulge of her shifts, revealing the soft bump of her nose and the unmistakable point of her sharp chin. Without warning, my skin puckers where her teeth gnash into me, sucking my flesh into her mouth like a leech. My peripheral vision whites out. Bright snapping sensations make sudden stars that blot out all sight. This little bitch always knew how to hurt me. I'm the one who taught her how.

I smell Cris before I see her. "I've always said you should meet my daughter."

"Bring her to a show, then."

"I did," I say, then ignore the confused cock of Cris's head.

"What about my money?"

"In my purse. Go grab it."

Cris grunts, mildly annoyed I don't have it in hand already. I stop her before she can get too far. "Enjoy this. It's probably the last time you'll ever be free."

"What is that supposed to mean?"

I realize my statement is one of those obscure things a young person just won't understand until they have a few more decades under their belt, so I don't elaborate. "One day you'll remember this night and realize I'm right. That's all."

Cris dismisses me with a wave. "Are you sure you can perform in your condition?"

"See that drink on the counter? It's yours. I've got to change."

As it happens, changing outfits is not easy with a seventeen-year-old girl swirling in your innards, but I was smart enough to pack clothes that stretch. Luckily, my entire wardrobe is already varying shades of black.

Showtime is a mere thirty minutes away. Right on schedule, my earlier calm has all but evaporated and been replaced by an anxiousness of unholy proportions. I am not nervous, but fidgety under the oppressive weight of this showtime limbo. I want to begin; then again, I don't.

I want something. An answer? I don't know. Some indication that these life implosions of mine have a meaning. That the losses and failures will all be worth it.

Once again, Cris has set up a keyboard for me to "speak" with the audience. I plan to speak continually for the entirety of the show. Not one letter, nor one song, will exist without my birthing it.

I don't know how long I wait in the back room, stoic as a smelly carob tree, before the front doors burst open. Excitable voices blast the quiet to smithereens, and before long I catch wind of an off-kilter chant.

Dis-co Ma-ma! Dis-co Ma-ma!

The energy of it swells to a roar. They want me. They want explanations. They want to be able to say they were here for Disco Mama's last show. Then, I blink and the chanting snaps out of reach, replaced with the regular murmur of a crowd. Perhaps I imagined it. Perhaps it's a premonition–the muting of my senses one by one as Regina Gayle Clark dies.

Cris meets me backstage. She takes one look at me and does her best to mask the concern dripping from her features.

"You good?" she asks. "Like, for real?"

"Can you hand me my mask from my bag?" Cris wipes the sweat from her hands on the front of her jeans and obliges my final request.

"What is it with the eyes on this thing?"

"You want to know the truth?"

Cris frowns, preparing to disbelieve anything I say. Her expression makes her look just like Lola.

I say, "I just thought they were neat. Nothing much to it beyond that."

Everything in place, she faces me. "You look like shit," she says.

"Then keep the stage dark."

She smiles, as assured as she is going to be. "When is your daughter coming?"

"Soon, probably. When you meet her, make sure you run like hell in the opposite direction."

"Why?"

I look past her, toward the stage. "I have a feeling she's going to be hungry."

My belly ripples from the friction of a vicious cackle—not mine, but Lola's. I feel her derision in my bones.

Before I disappear completely, I turn to Cris and say, "Never leave your house without a weapon, kid. You never know who the baddies are."

She tries to ask me what the fuck I'm talking about, but I'm gone.

Originally, I anticipated sneaking onto the stage in the dark and letting Cris gradually reveal me under dark red lights, but I changed my mind at the last minute. Instead, we don't announce anything, offering no indication that the show is to begin. I storm directly to center stage: no pomp, no circumstance, no nothing. Just me and my seething stare, demanding the room to quiet.

And they do. Once I'm spotted, the entire crowd faces me in domino fashion. Their lips purse shut except to hammer down more liquor. They hush, they stare, I stare back, and we hold vigil there together for ten, maybe fifteen seconds.

Cris's cue is my first sentence: *Want to know who Disco Mama really is?* She drops the lights to black and so I can blow out their eardrums and really get their attention.

I shuffle about in front of my controller, a real nice one that I charged to my credit card a week ago, a monstrous charge that will accelerate Jimothy's stroke trajectory tenfold, and I adjust myself to its new features while Lola churns within me, as if she can sense how much I crave this moment and has been saving all her energy just to fuck it up.

She jabs me something fierce. As I'm typing our starting cue, and just as the lights wick away, Lola doubles me over in pain. Fine, little brat, I needed to grab her shitty boyfriend's skull from the purse at my feet anyway.

The audience begins to hoot. They're buzzing. Someone shouts out, "Fuck yeah!" because of course they want to know who I am, and, more importantly, what I've done. That's the only reason they're here.

Then, the music hits. A blaring siren devolves into the steady beat of my intro song. Before the lights return, I set Calvin's skull on top of my table so his soulless eyes are the first thing the crowd sees as Cris works her magic.

As the lights ascend floor-to-ceiling, so does the noise. I can't tell if the audience notices the skull because I'm already assaulting their senses with music loud enough to shake the Richter scale. The music–the vibrating bass blowing holes in my eardrums–is everything I need. The heat of injury radiates from my entire midsection in time with the beat. It's the sharp pain only caused by pointed objects. I have little time to wonder what Lola is up to before she hits me with it again, harder. This injury doesn't double me over, but that could be because my attention is already somewhere else, hovering over the scalps of the crowd, in the rafters, as if my consciousness aerosolized with the music, like I'm nothing more than a molecule among the sound. It's perfect; I love it here. I never want to leave.

Lola continues to mercilessly pummel me in cadence with my carefully planned crescendos. The music fuels her vitality just as much as it does mine, like she's harnessing the wonder of it into her balled up and furious fists. No one can see her or feel her like I can. No one else understands how sincere this moment is between us–perhaps our only one, ever. I find myself wishing I'd done everything differently. Carried away by the sound of the moment, my mind drifts to past Saturday mornings, of good coffee and my husband drawing his fingers over my shoulders as he passes by the table. Nothing to do but laze around and be together, and right then is the only time in my forty-five years where I enjoy living. Which is also exactly when I realize that this is what had gone wrong this entire time: I hated everything about my life but did nothing to change or improve it, did nothing but lament my poor choices. I have always been a lazy person. Even Disco Mama will never last, never. I'll get bored and drift away from her, devouring everyone in my orbit whole until they're just an empty void of existence.

It's funny, really. Lola kicks my sternum again and I lose my breath, but not my amusement. The sheer absurdity of this moment is spectacular. It can never be surpassed because I've engineered it that way. In a way, I'm the luckiest motherfucker alive.

So I type–

DON'T DROP THE SKULL!

My words scroll on the projector behind me with seconds to spare before I toss Calvin's head into a frothing pit of drunks and dancers. Their faces are open, mouths open and hungry. They are baby birds waiting for Mother's digested filth.

MEET MY DAUGHTER'S BOYFRIEND.
I KILLED HIM WITH A SEATBELT.

The part of the crowd here for "vibes only" screams at the top of their lungs. If Disco Mama killed some drummer or not, they don't give a shit. Other pearl-clutching fools hold their palms over shocked, gaping mouths. It's all the same though, these vultures, these macabre dumpster-diving parasites, they're all the same–intrigue, horror, and suspense, that's all they're here for. The connecting thread is that none of them know for sure if I'm telling the truth, which means they'll hang onto my every movement searching for answers.

And then they'll call *me* the monster.

YOU'LL NEVER FIND HIS BODY.
TEAR ME APART TO GET IT.

More screaming. I've lost sight of the skull, but that's okay. Internally, I bid Calvin goodbye and return my focus to the show. Within me, Lola stretches her arms with enough force to crack a rib. The sickening snap of it nearly drops me to my knees, but I'm quick to recover.

DON'T MIND ME. I'M IN LABOR.

There is far less enthusiasm for this comment, and there are noticeable pockets of stoic attendees (cops?) as the merriment of dancing wanes. This perplexes me at first until I understand that I've never held a room's attentive captive with as much power as I do now.

I type:

TURN UP THE HOUSE LIGHTS.

Then, I crank the noise and redline the shit out of everything. I want to make their ears bleed. I want their lifelong tinnitus to bring them right back to this night. To me and my show.

The room gasps as the lights pull up, all eyes zeroed onto my heaving stomach. Lola writhes so ferociously that even the people in the back can spot her body moving under my clothes. My skin bobs and stretches, alien-like. I am inhuman, another entity, and they can do nothing but gaze upon my ungodliness–for what is a God but the unknown? And believe me, they do not know me.

IT'S NEARLY TIME

Lola steals my breath with every stretch. She's back with whatever needle she's found in there, cutting through me from the inside out. She is the puppeteer. She's got me by the nerves, and my body behaves like a wet sack of meat and reacts to her whims. Every time I try to move myself one way, Lola tugs me in the other direction so that my movements are uncontrollable spasms, seizure-like and haunted. I am possessed, and I look like it too.

Someone screams quietly, as if they'd tried to hush themselves but failed, an involuntary shudder of horror. Fighting the searing pain in my torso, I will my hands to my keyboard for one last statement, as I threaten my daughter under my breath.

"You know, Emily came to see me."

She stills for a second, just long enough for me to type:

CHECK MY GARAGE FOR THE REST OF THEM

Then, I break into an epileptic cackle that originates from my bowels and lands like rot into the audience. I can't take it anymore, none of this, the boredom of existing. What more can I do before I eat myself alive?

The screams of the audience surge from confusion to something feral as I distort myself for their pleasure. This is what they came for and they'll never admit it, but I am part of them now. Lola and I are one, and we will haunt them until they die.

"See you in your fucking dreams!" I scream into their faces before I keel over and retch out one of Lola's bracelets onto the stage. Blood and viscera are curled within its plastic beads, and the crowd's screaming becomes insatiable, and I hear feet and pounding, pure terror and dismay, and God is it so delicious, so delicious I might eat up that jewelry a second time. My torso is on fire–Lola with her sharpened knife, her own rib, her blade. My skin flexes under her weapon like a nylon balloon poked by fingers, and I'm on my knees dry heaving from pain, how lovely, how pure pain can be, which is when I finally see it–the small looped metal of an earring jutting free of its flesh enclosure, and a pink and bloodied hand following it, and I can't speak, only watch as my psyche floats away to observe my dying body from above as Lola bursts out of me like a parasite too big for its host. She is peeling me like a banana, one piece of me shredded to pulp as the other drowns in my own blood, appendages twitching my body, my glassy eyes catching sight of my beautiful and wretched child screaming at the top of her lungs at the audience, at me, at the universe.

She turns to me, and as my senses fail, she howls, "What *now*, you fucking bitch!"

My last words are not "I love you." I tell her to eat all those people alive, every last one of them. Or I think I do. I hope I do. I can't feel my body or my fingers anymore. I'm cold and everything is dark.

But my life does not flash before my eyes. Instead, I return to my daughter like an inhaled infection. I see her.

I am her. We are so goddamn hungry. The hot blood of youth flows through me, pumping vigorously through the shared heart of our bodies, mother and daughter.

I am not dead. Lola will carry me with her wherever she goes.

Try and catch us now, motherfuckers.

ACKNOWLEDGEMENTS

I want to thank my family for putting up with me, and supporting me for years. Without you all, and you know who you are, I probably would have given up a long time ago.

To all the people who I've crossed paths with in my bookish travels, thank you. So many of you have enriched my life and made me a better person just by knowing you. If you're reading this and wondering if I mean you, I promise I do. There are just too many of you to properly name without making this a phonebook directory.

Finally, this book would simply not exist without FZ. Your unyielding belief in my work is all that kept me writing for a while. This book is as much yours as it is mine, and I am grateful every day for your patience, revisions, and profound insight. From the bottom of my curmudgeonly heart, thank you.